Penguin Books
Scars on the Soul

Françoise Sagan was born in 1935 and took
her *nom de plume* from the Princesse de Sagan
of Marcel Proust. She was eighteen years old
when she wrote her best-selling *Bonjour Tristesse*.
She had failed to pass her examinations at the
Sorbonne and decided to write a novel. The
book received great acclaim in France, where
in 1959 it had sold 850,000 copies, and also
abroad. Her second and third books, *A Certain
Smile* and *Those Without Shadows*, have also had
tremendous popularity in France, Great
Britain and the U.S.A. These were followed by
Aimez-vous Brahms . . . (1959), *Wonderful Clouds*
(1961), *La Chamade* (1965), *The Heart-Keeper*
(1968) and *Sunlight on Cold Water* (1971). Her
most recent novels are *Lost Profile* and *Le Lit défait* and a
collection of stories, *Silken Eyes*, all to be published in Penguin.

Françoise Sagan is married and has a son.

Françoise Sagan

Scars on the Soul

Translated from the French
by Joanna Kilmartin

Penguin Books

Penguin Books Ltd, Harmondsworth,
Middlesex, England
Penguin Books, 625 Madison Avenue,
New York, New York 10022, U.S.A.
Penguin Books Australia Ltd, Ringwood,
Victoria, Australia
Penguin Books Canada Ltd, 2801 John Street,
Markham, Ontario, Canada L3R 1B4
Penguin Books (N.Z.) Ltd, 182–190 Wairau Road,
Auckland 10, New Zealand

Des Bleus à l'âme first published by Flammarion 1972
This translation first published by André Deutsch, Limited 1974
Published in Penguin Books 1977

Copyright © Flammarion, 1972
This edition copyright © Françoise Sagan, 1977
This translation copyright © André Deutsch Limited, 1974
All rights reserved

Made and printed in Great Britain by
Cox & Wyman Ltd, London, Reading and Fakenham
Set in Intertype Baskerville

To Charlotte Aillaud

I have said that the soul is not more than the body,
And I have said that the body is not more than the soul,
And nothing, not God, is greater to one than one's self is,
And whoever walks a furlong without sympathy walks
to his own funeral drest in his shroud . . .

WALT WHITMAN, *Song of Myself*

Chapter One

March 1971

I should like to have written: 'Sebastian went up the stairs four at a time, puffing and blowing a little.' I should have enjoyed resurrecting those characters of ten years ago, Sebastian and his sister Eleanor – characters in a play, of course, but a light-hearted play, one of mine – depicting them flat broke but still gay, cynical and fastidious, trying in vain to 'recoup' in a Paris depressed by its own mediocrity. Unfortunately, the mediocrity of Paris, or my own, has got the better of my crazier whims, and today I'm painfully trying to remember how and when 'it' began. 'It' being the revulsion, the boredom, the distaste I now feel for a way of life that until now, and for very good reasons, had always attracted me. More, I think it was in 1969 and I don't think, alas, that the events of 1968, the elation and the letdown, had much to do with it. Or age either. I'm thirty-five, my teeth are good, and if I feel attracted to someone, on the whole it still works. Except that I'm no longer interested. I'd like to be in love and even to suffer and even to tremble at the sound of the telephone. Or to play the same record ten times running and wake in the mornings with that feeling of natural euphoria I used to take for granted. 'They took away my taste for water, now they've taken away my taste for love.' That's from a Jacques Brel record, I think. Anyway, I can't seem to function any longer and I even doubt whether I'll show this to my publisher. It isn't literature, it isn't a true confession, it's someone tapping away at her typewriter because she's afraid of herself and the typewriter and the mornings and the evenings and everything else. And of other people. Fear isn't very nice; in fact, it's rather shameful, and I've never felt it before. That's all. But that 'all' terrifies me.

I'm not alone in my plight. In this spring of 1971 in Paris, everyone I see or hear seems unsettled, frightened. Perhaps death is prowling around us and we sense it and are tormenting ourselves about nothing. For after all, that's not the problem. Death – I'm not talking about illness – death, to me, is velvet-clad, gloved, black, and in any case irremediable, absolute. And I yearn for the absolute as I did at fifteen. But the sad thing is that I've experienced enough of life's pleasures to know that, for me, this notion of the absolute can only be a step backwards, a confession of weakness – that I force myself to look upon as purely temporary. Out of pride, no doubt, and once again, out of fear. My death is the least of evils.

No, it's the perpetual, the ubiquitous violence, the misunderstandings, the anger, so often justified, the loneliness, the sense of rushing headlong towards disaster. It's the young who refuse to accept – having had it flung in their faces so often – that they'll lose their youth one day, and the 'mature' people who for the past three years have fought tooth and nail against growing older and are now floundering. And the women who want equality with men, and the good arguments and the good faith of some and the grotesque obtuseness of others, human just the same and subject to the same god, the only god, whom they try to deny: Time. But who reads Proust?

And the new jargon, and the difficulty of communicating, and the milk of human kindness, springing up from time to time. Rarely though. And occasionally a face to admire. And life, mad life. I've always thought of it as a savage she-wolf, crazily maternal. Bloody mama, Jocasta, Leah, all rolled into one, and always, of course, in the end, Medea. Flinging us down here, on a planet which it now seems – oh, final affront – is not even unique; and when I say 'affront' I mean 'affront', since ours, after all, was supposed to be the only life, the only thought, the only music, the only history. And what if there were others? What if our mother, that lying adulteress, had had other children, elsewhere? When man, Apollo man, rockets into space, it isn't in order to find his brother, I'm quite sure of that. It's to confirm that he hasn't any brothers, that the miserable three score years and ten which she has given him are his and his alone. One has only to look at the Martians of popular imagination. Why are they always small and ugly? Because we're jealous. Then again: 'There's no grass on the moon, is there?' No, 'grass belongs to us.' And the whole of this good earth of ours, so chauvinistic, so terror-stricken, relaxes and at once starts cheerfully tearing itself apart, snatching the grass from its mouth or soaking it in blood, in the same equally senseless impulse.

And all those cretins who concern themselves with 'the people', who talk about 'the people' with such pathetic awkwardness in their left-wing garb and exhaust us in the end because of the trouble we have to take, those of us who detest the Right, to protect them, to prevent some raging (or, for that matter, docile) lunatic from really reducing that wretched garb to unwearable rags. The people. Unaware that the very word is insulting, that there's a man plus a man plus a woman plus a child plus a man, etc., that each individual is wholly distinct in everything, even in his deepest aspirations, and that as a rule, for lack of means, this individual will be able neither to hear nor to see nor to read them. Sartre, when he climbed on to his tub, awkwardly, honestly, perhaps understood. And Diogenes, from the interior of his tub, speaking to all and sundry. It's people such as they, who are compassionate and have the intelligence of their compassion, that are held up to ridicule. But what do they care? In our day it's a noble thing, ridicule, *being*

9

ridiculed, for a keen mind. Noble and disquieting – because noble. Neither Stendhal nor Balzac would have borne it. (In their work, of course.) For me, the only prophet in this respect was Dostoevsky.

Here I've been talking about life instead of about the debonair and desperate Swedish aristocrat, Sebastian van Milhem. But who knows? He may re-emerge and I'll talk about his affairs. It's my job, after all; I write, I enjoy writing, and I make a very good living out of it. It seems to me that life, in its female-animal aspect, carries some of its offspring around by the scruff of the neck like a wise and gentle mother cat (which assures you a reasonably comfortable existence). And some by the small of the back, in which precarious position, seeking a fall as a blessed release, many of our contemporaries find themselves. Or by one paw, and never mind the lovesick, the hopelessly trapped, the seriously ill, and a few of the poets. Never mind them. But that's absurd. I shall always mind about poetry; it's the one thing I've always loved and never known how to write.

And yet I would readily conjure up even the smell of grass and scatter a basketful of dried and scented grasses through the pages of this cynical novel. Now that I'm reduced to this: naming things. For the smell of grass, when I stretch myself out in it, bury my face in it, is something I now feel obliged to name myself: this is the smell of grass, Madame. As for the sea, the crazy sea, I have to introduce my body to it, too: this is your best friend, the sea. My body acknowledges it, but doesn't rush to greet it. I'm a long-suffering mother at a watering place, dragging along a fractious child: her own body. 'Say good morning to Madame Dupont, who was so kind to you when she was taking the cure here last year (or ten years ago).' And the fractious child recoils. Recoils, sometimes, at the very suggestion of love and its enchantments. As my eyes recoil, horrified, from those magazine advertisements in glorious technicolour, in which limpid seas lap against red rocks and miles upon miles of impeccable beaches are displayed, all for 1,300 frs. return. 'Oh, let them go,' sighs my fascist body, 'let them all go, let them get their suntans and have their fun in those places that were so often the century and the love of my life, my special territory. Let them keep them, for that matter. Long live the Club Méditerranée. Down with the sea of that name! Let her, poor fool, frolic with her young executives, her not-so-young executives, her campers! Personally, I shall sing her praises no more, I shall put her out of my mind; and if I should happen to be passing at some suitable moment, in April, say, I'll dip a toe or a chilly, listless hand. She and I, who once upon a time . . .' How sad! That's what growing old must be: no longer recognizing one's nearest and dearest. And what shall I say of all those other bodies that have accompanied mine, side by side, over the past fifteen years, to which I would return from time to time to sleep or to unwind, and which I now shun as though I were suddenly imprisoned once more in what Éluard called 'that thin, proud body, wild bird body, creature of my childhood'.

Chapter Two

Sebastian ran up the stairs four at a time, puffing and blowing a little. He was beginning to find the sixth floor a bit high for him. It wasn't his weight that bothered him, but ten thousand cigarettes in the past few years and an equal number of drinks, the very variety of which made him laugh. In fact, he might almost have distinguished the past few years one from another by his favourite drinks rather than his women. There had been Negroni year, which corresponded to Hedda's year, and Dry Martini year which, though longer, coincided with Mariella Della. And Rum year, in Brazil, with Anne-Marie. My God, what fun he'd had! Not that, all things considered, he was a heavy drinker or even a womanizer, though he delighted in the combination of a woman and a drink. In any case, his sister Eleanor was the sole mistress of his existence, his sister, and in her case without alcohol or with every sort of alcohol. Life without her, drink without her, were like lukewarm water. Not a bad thing, all said and done, to have one's life circumscribed to that extent by someone who – whatever she might say – was as much his slave as he was hers. From time to time she would become restive, marry, disappear, and then, after a few chaotic months, a few embroilments about which she would only tell him much later – but with what hilarious giggles – she would come back to him. Rich or poor, exhausted or bursting with health, melancholy or gay, the wild, the incomparable, the beautiful Eleanor, his sister, would always come back to him.

On this occasion, they had just arrived together from a long stay in Scandinavia with one of Eleanor's husbands, and their circumstances looked bad. It was only by a miraculous chance that an old friend of Sebastian's had lent them this two-room flat in the Rue de Fleurus. And they could hardly have had much money either in the bank or in their pockets. Eleanor would willingly have handed over her two or three splendid pieces of jewellery, since possessions meant nothing to her, but to what purpose? In any case, jewellery was an asset to a woman.

Sebastian rang their bell and she opened the door at once, in her dressing-gown.

'Oh, you poor boy,' she said, helping him to a rickety chair. 'Oh, you poor boy, puffing up the stairs at your age. I could hear you coming up and was afraid you mightn't make it.'

He put his hand on his heart, feigning exhaustion.

'I'm getting old,' he said.

'What about me?' she laughed. 'At the bottom of those stairs I'm Isadora Duncan, I positively float. By the time I reach the top, I'm more like Fats Domino. Did you find someone?'

'Someone' being that providential person who, because of their charm, their wit, their luck, would act as temporary provider for brother and sister. This person had so far never failed to materialize and was usually discovered by Sebastian, Eleanor, as in this case, being too lazy to go out.

'Not a soul,' said Sebastian. 'Arturo is in the Argentine, the Villavers are on holiday; and believe it or not, Nicholas is working.'

A look of doubt and slight horror appeared in Eleanor's eyes. (Work had never been a strong point with the van Milhems.)

'What a town,' she said. 'Mind you, there's one good thing: it doesn't matter what I wear. The big couturiers are out; a curtain, trousers, a bit of my jewellery on smart occasions, anything goes. You've only got to look around you in the streets. As long as I don't forget I'm thirty-nine, I'm safe. In any case, I shan't be the only one.'

'Just as well,' Sebastian said, 'but I always knew you'd have nothing to worry about.'

It was true: with her immensely long legs, her lean, muscular body, her well-defined features, high cheekbones, clear, almond-shaped eyes, Eleanor was still superb to look at. As for him, underlying his habitual, quizzical expression, he had the same bone structure as his sister. No, they'd get by all right. He stretched out his legs.

'The tiresome thing is, apparently there's a shortage of men around the place. I'm going to have to do my bit, sooner than you, probably.'

'It serves you right,' she said. 'But how do you know?'

'Nicholas told me. It seems that lots of men, fed up with their wives, have taken to making love to one another, and the town's overrun by baying women in search of prey. And *they've* no sooner quieted down, than the students take over. Ah, parasitism is no longer what it was.'

'No obscenities. Look how beautiful Paris is.'

He leaned on the window sill beside her. A pink light suffused the wall opposite and glinted off the surrounding rooftops. A smell of fresh earth rose from the Luxembourg Gardens, overpowering the petrol fumes. He laughed.

'If you're going to wear a curtain, I suppose I can let my hair grow?'

'Hurry up, then. It'll soon start falling out.'

He gave her a brotherly kick on the ankle. He no longer had a care in the world.

Perhaps I should turn the story of my two cuckoos into a play after all. So far, this hardly resembles the beginning of a novel. Perhaps I ought to have – what's the word? – 'placed' my characters, described the setting. The setting, especially, is pretty minimal. But settings bore me, except by a few writers who take such meticulous, delectable pleasure in them that I find myself smiling in sympathy. Now there, admittedly, rereading what I've written, it doesn't amount to much: six floors, a rickety chair, rooftops (that makes sense on the sixth floor). In fact, the modest and precarious circumstances of my protagonists seem to me amply described by those six flights of stairs. I've always loathed stairs: I get out of breath going up and vertigo coming down. (I once gave someone up because he lived on the fifth floor. He never knew why.) If by attributing my personal dislikes to the van Milhems I'm leaving them in an empty apartment, so be it. They're gay and carefree, and that's the best of décors. Especially as I'm going to have to find someone to feed them, and someone who isn't ludicrously conventional, at that. Where, I don't know: the rich are always wailing about having no money, the poor haven't any but say so more quietly, and then there's income tax, etc. It'll have to be a foreigner. That's what we've come to in France in 1971. For the sake of verisimilitude, I'm going to be compelled to have my delightful van Milhems supported by a foreigner. Preferably domiciled in Switzerland. It's very wounding for my national pride. Moreover, I can't put Eleanor to work in Marie-Martine or a ready-to-wear shop. That would be like launching Sebastian into banking or the Stock Exchange. It would be the death of them both. Contrary to general belief, idleness is as powerful a drug as work. Prevent a hard worker from doing his job, and he'll go into a decline, become depressed, lose weight, and so on. But your truly lazy man, after a few weeks' work, will also fall into a state of 'deprivation'. He'll go into a decline, become depressed, lose weight, and the rest. I've no intention of killing Sebastian and Eleanor with work. I've often been taken to task because my little circle is idle and blasé and this and that; but that's no reason to sacrifice my two languid Swedes on the altar of criticism. I'll think about it later on, with different characters, in another book (God and my publisher permitting). Some day I'll write about pay envelopes, car instalment payments, television, and normal people. If there are any left. Considering what we inflict on them. I know people who have cars like little metal boxes and secretly enjoy sitting in traffic jams in the middle of this dear old familiar pollution. They're happy to take an hour or an hour and a half between their homes and their offices. Because, for one whole hour, they're *alone* in their little boxes. They're safe from company, from conversation, from 'aggression', as the psychiatrists would say. But just try getting a man or a woman who goes out to work to admit it: the car as refuge, igloo, womb, etc. No, in my view, what men spend their Sundays polishing with a special cloth isn't an instrument of aggression, it's their privacy, their one luxury.

Beware of gaiety. I distrust that insidious euphoria which, after a difficult beginning, grips a writer at the end of two or three chapters and has him muttering to himself: 'Hurray, machinery's getting going again!' or 'Hurray, we're off!' Innocent mechanic's phrases, true, but occasionally followed by: 'Hurray, I won't have to commit suicide after all.' (A more poetic observation, but sometimes true.) That's how the creator goes off the rails, distinguishing himself, by this abrupt change of key, from his classmates, the rest of humanity. Such euphoria is dangerous, because you believe you've 'laid the foundations' (these constant references to manual jobs), and in these circumstances, the worst terror behind you, what's wrong with a bit of a breather? Especially if Deauville, deserted and bathed in the slanting yellow sunlight of March, is on your doorstep. I could understand, the other day, looking at those black, solitary buildings against the bright sky, at the decorously abandoned sea (we've never had a very passionate relationship, the Channel and I, for reasons of temperature), I could understand why all the young film directors drag their cameras and their heroes there in winter. I thought to myself then that I couldn't bear another film sequence of a man and a woman running along a beach, any more than I could bear yet another shot of two people (or a dozen), regardless of their sex, naked in bed with the sheet pulled back. Here and now, I should warn anyone who wants titillation that there won't be a trace of it in this novel. At the most: 'Eleanor didn't come home that night.' But it's true, isn't it! What's become of night's wild delights, the whispered words in the dark, the 'secrecy', the profound secrecy of physical love? Where is the violence, the beauty, the dignity of pleasure? You see a woman with her eyes closed twisting her head from left to right on a pillow, and the silhouette of some poor fellow's muscled back jerking rhythmically, and you wait placidly in your cinema seat for them to get it over. You begin to envy people who can be shocked by this; at least they're being entertained. What a bore it is, this mass, this tonnage of human flesh, tanned or pallid, standing, sitting, or lying, which is shoved under our noses these days! The body and its pleasures have become consumer goods, like everything else. Poor things, thinking they've overcome stupid prejudices when in fact they've ruined a splendid mythology. There are moments when I'm on the point of writing, 'But I digress,' an old-fashioned courtesy to the reader, but pointless in this case, since my purpose is to digress. Nevertheless, this blow-by-blow account of eroticism has irritated me. I'm returning to my van Milhems, 'who frequently indulge in that sort of thing, but never talk about it.'

Chapter Three

The restaurant was excellent. Eleanor had ordered nine oysters, which writhed visibly under the impact of the lemon juice, a grilled sole, and a bottle of very dry Pouilly Fuissé. Sebastian, who was hungrier, had tucked away an *œuf en gelée* and a *steak au poivre* (the real thing), washed down with Beaujolais. There was no *vin de Bouzy*, a fact which they momentarily deplored. Contrary to her predictions, Eleanor wasn't dressed in a curtain. Waving some magic wand which she alone seemed to possess, she had run into an old girl-friend of the kind every woman dreams of, plain, devoted, and efficient, who had taken her off to a ready-to-wear shop run by a man she knew, where one could order things on credit. Fascinated by Eleanor, this man had there and then designed several dresses for her, waving aside her offer, admittedly sheer braggadocio, to give him a cheque. And lo and behold, it was a sumptuously dressed Eleanor who was now guzzling Sebastian's (and therefore her own) last remaining nine thousand old francs on the terrace of a *brasserie* in the Rue Marbœuf.

'After this lunch, according to my calculations, we'll have about three thousand francs left,' Sebastian said, screwing up his eyes against the sun. 'You're sure you don't want anything else? In that case, we've got enough for a taxi.'

'It doesn't make sense,' Eleanor said. 'If I'd eaten one of those pastries, a taxi would have been a virtual necessity to get me home. Life is badly arranged.'

They smiled at one another. In the harsh spring sunlight,

tiny wrinkles were clearly visible on both of their faces. *Dear Eleanor,* thought Sebastian, *dear Eleanor, I'll get you out of this somehow.* Sudden emotion brought a lump to his throat and made him speechless.

'Your steak was too peppery,' said Eleanor absently, 'you've got tears in your eyes.'

She had lowered her eyes. Was she telling herself that they were nothing but a pair of good-for-nothings in a town which suddenly seemed alien, bustling, indifferent to the charms and the lures of the van Milhems? True, men were looking at her, but to see and be seen they should have been at Maxim's or the Plaza-Athénée. And his suit was hardly smart enough for that. He finished his wine at a gulp.

'Tonight,' Eleanor said thoughtfully, 'we'll buy a can of ravioli. I adore ravioli. Then, if it wouldn't bore you, and if you know how to work your friend's radio, we'll listen to the Champs-Élysées concert. It's being broadcast live. We'll open the window, it'll be marvellous.'

'What are they playing?'

'Mahler, Schubert, Strauss. I looked this morning. What a delicious lunch, Sebastian.'

She stretched out her long arms, her slim hands in front of her in a gesture of contentment. A man behind her noticed the gesture and Sebastian, amused, saw him grow pale with desire. He had in fact been staring at Eleanor from the moment she entered the room, with a bright, unblinking gaze that finally embarrassed Sebastian, sitting facing him. He wore a shabby suit and a frightful tie and had a briefcase beside him. Doubtless some local bank clerk with a mild obsession about women. But the innocence of his stare suggested something more. A touch of madness, perhaps. Moreover, when they got up to leave, he got up too, as though he had been sharing their table, and at his first sight of Eleanor's face, gave her a furtive childlike look that took her aback.

'His eyes never once left the back of your neck,' Sebastian said, seeing his sister's look of surprise. 'Shall we walk a bit, or go straight home?'

'I'm dying to finish my book,' she said.

She would lose herself in books, sometimes for a whole day, and the devoted girl-friend had discovered a lending library in the neighbourhood, whose owner was quickly charmed into assuaging Eleanor's insatiable literary hunger. She read anything and everything, stretched out on the sofa or on her bed, sometimes for hours on end, while Sebastian wandered in and out, chatted to the locals in the bar around the corner or the keepers in the Luxembourg Gardens, and trained himself to plod methodically up the six flights of stairs. Tonight, after the ravioli and Mahler, this idyllic existence must come to an end. A thought that filled him with quiet despair.

Still no solution for the van Milhems. Impossible to find easy money in Paris just now, even for them. The intrusion of the fixated clerk, which I hadn't foreseen, intrigues me. What am I to do with him? Eleanor has a horror of crackpots, if I remember rightly. Anyway, I'd like to point out to my faithful readers that it's the first time in eighteen years of novel writing that I've offered them a menu. A real menu. Oysters, fish, etc. And wine. Even an approximate price. I can see I shall end up by writing interminable novels stuffed with detail. Just watch me describe a house, the exterior, the interior, the colour of the curtains, the style of the furniture, the grandfather's features, the granddaughter's dress, the smell of the attic, the ritual at mealtimes, the place settings, the glasses, the tablecloths and, to round it all off, something like: 'There now arrived, on a bed of bay leaves, surrounded by blood-red tomatoes and pimentos, a dead carp, whose grey skin, flaking off here and there, further accentuated its dazzling whiteness.' Perhaps that's where happiness lies, for a writer. No more light music – on with the brass band! While I'm on the subject of light music, a second warning to the unfortunate – and I hope faithful – reader: just as there will be no smut in this book, neither will there be the least trace of autobiography, not a single amusing anecdote about Saint-Tropez vintage '54, nothing about my way of life, my friends, and so forth. For two reasons. The more important, in my view, being that it's nobody's business but mine. And secondly, once I embark on facts, my imagination – truly the mad boarder* – will lead me astray, distorting my account in favour of anything that appeals to my sense of the ridiculous. By avoiding the particular, I shan't be in danger of lying. The worst I shall do is get my quotations wrong. Amen. But in all good faith.

It would be comic, however, if this good faith (mine), so often the despair of journalists – and how I sympathize with them (Dali's interviews fill me with glee) – it would be amusing if this good faith, this placid, bovine creature I've been dragging around with me since the day I was born (I'm speaking, of course, about general topics), were suddenly to have become, with all the *muletas* waved in front of its muzzle – Israel, Russia, Poland, the New Novel, Youth, the Middle East, Communism, Solzhenitsyn, the Americans, Vietnam, etc – if this poor beast, incapable of munching and assimilating the fodder necessary to its growth and its understanding of a world in which, after all, I drag out an existence like everyone else, were to have become the maddened bull which goads me into writing this eccentric book in fits and starts. A reckless bull, 'at once broken-hearted and stony-hearted' (to paraphrase Chamfort).† Not that I wish to rip apart my *picadors* – the men who claim to have all the answers and in fact have nothing of the kind, poor things,

* *La folle du logis*, Malebranche.

† '*En vivant et en voyant les hommes, il faut que le coeur se brise ou se bronze.*' Chamfort.

but go on blowing their trumpets nonetheless. They're my friends, of course. My enemies have been crying wolf, or Jew, or nigger, or what have you ever since I can remember. The *picadors* I mean are those who still pay lip service to the dove democracy, that freedom which is so precious to them – and to me, for that matter – but which I, for one, am beginning to suspect would prefer to leave its feathers in their over-enthusiastic hands and fly away naked into the blue, rather than perch anywhere in the world at present. Even if, on her return, homesick for our loving words, she is nearly shot to pieces by those who imitate our voices. When I say 'our', I mean only those poor fools who don't regard themselves as a matter of course as judges or as experts. There aren't many left, I'm afraid. Let's get back to our Swedes, let's smother them in silk, gold, and mazurkas. The unrhythmical 'jerks' (first on one foot, then on the other) of our political leaders and thinkers exasperate me. Let's forget them.

Chapter Four

The concert had been very enjoyable, even though Eleanor had let the ravioli burn and Sebastian had been left with slight hunger pangs which he tried to appease with cigarettes. The window was still open to the night air and Eleanor still sitting on the floor, half turned away from him, so that he could see only her profile, so familiar and so remote, calmly turned towards the night. *The only woman I've ever wanted to ask: what are you thinking about?* he reflected. And also the only one who would never have told him.

The telephone rang, making them jump. No one knew they were there, on their island in the Latin Quarter, and Sebastian hesitated a moment before answering it. Then he picked up the receiver gingerly; he sensed that life was about to call them to order, in the nick of time for their finances, maybe, but too soon for their peace of mind. *Why shouldn't they just kill themselves here and now,* he thought, *after forty years of good and loyal service in the cause of living?* He knew that Eleanor, though not remotely suicidal, would have joined him.

'Hello?' said a voice, male but high-pitched. 'Is that you, Robert?'

'Robert Bessy is away,' Sebastian said politely. 'He should be back any day now.'

'In that case, who're you?' asked the voice.

People's manners certainly haven't improved, thought Sebastian. He made an effort to control himself.

'He was kind enough to lend me his flat while he was away.'

'Then you must be Sebastian. How marvellous! Robert's always talking about you. Listen, I wanted to ask him to the opening of a new club tonight – very smart, very amusing. The Jedelmans ... Do you know the Jedelmans? Would it amuse you to come along?'

Sebastian looked inquiringly at Eleanor. The voice was reverberating as if through a loud-speaker.

'I'm afraid I don't know your name,' Sebastian said cautiously.

'Gilbert. Gilbert Benoit. Are you game, then? Here's the address ...'

'I'm staying here with my sister,' Sebastian cut in. 'I should think we could be ready in half an hour, but we wouldn't dream of going by ourselves, without knowing Monsieur and Madame ...?'

'Jedelman,' babbled the voice. 'But it's a club, and ...'

'Jedelman, good. Can you pick us up at the Rue de Fleurus in half an hour or would you prefer us to meet you later on?'

Eleanor, bright-eyed, was watching him. He was playing his cards damn well, for they had literally not enough money for a taxi, a bottle of Chianti having slipped in alongside the can of ravioli at the grocer's, as though of its own accord.

'I'll be waiting down below,' said the voice. 'Of course. It hadn't occurred to me ...'

'By the way,' Sebastian said, 'my name is Sebastian van Milhem and my sister's is Eleanor van Milhem. I mention this because of the introductions you'll have to make. See you shortly.'

He hung up and burst out laughing. Eleanor was grinning up at him.

'Who on earth are the Jedelmans?'

'God knows. The rich love to go slumming these days. They all want their own club. What are you going to wear?'

'My sea-green dress, I think. Make yourself beautiful,

brother dear, you may find yourself having to do your bit in more ways than one.'

He looked at her.

'Well, if the photographs in my room and Gilbert's voice are anything to go by, it looks as though your kind friend, our host, is as queer as could be.'

'Fool that I am!' exclaimed Sebastian, aghast. 'You're right, I'd completely forgotten. What a prospect!'

Two hours later, they were sitting at a large, noisy table, Sebastian's knee being sought from time to time by that of the rich Mme Jedelman, who was no longer in the first flush of youth. But still, she was massaged, showered, lacquered, manicured, and Sebastian thought philosophically that he had seen worse. Eleanor, on the other hand, seemed somewhat exasperated with her neighbour. After the minor sensation caused by their arrival (where had they sprung from, and who were they, these two blond strangers, so tall and so aloof, a brother and sister into the bargain?), Gilbert, delighted with his 'catch', had escorted them to the table of honour. M. Jedelman, apparently weary of his wife's caprices, had had to be taken home, dead drunk, at eleven o'clock. Two film stars, a singer, a famous woman gossip-columnist, and an unknown man made up Mme Jedelman's table, around which the photographers fluttered like moths. Gilbert did his best to answer questions about the van Milhems, but as he knew nothing whatsoever about them except the fact that Robert had been Sebastian's lifelong and unconditional admirer, he took refuge in an air of mystification, if not insinuation, which irritated everybody.

'No, monsieur,' said Eleanor's voice suddenly, and Sebastian pricked up his ears. 'No, I haven't seen all those films.'

'But that's incredible. You mean to say you've never heard of *Bonnie and Clyde*?'

The indignant cinema buff appealed to the rest of the table.

'She claims . . .'

'Madame,' interrupted Eleanor silkily, 'Madame claims.'

'Madame claims,' the poor man continued with a laugh, 'that she's never heard of *Bonnie and Clyde*.'

'As I've already told you, monsieur, I've been living in Sweden for ten years in a snowbound castle. My husband didn't possess a private cinema for showing films 'at home', as you put it. And we never went near Stockholm. That's all there is to it.'

There was a sudden silence; Eleanor's voice, without having been raised, had become distinctly sharp.

'You're getting cross, my sweet,' said Sebastian.

'It's so exhausting to repeat the same thing over and over again and to listen to the same thing over and over again.'

'I apologize, I apologize over and over again,' said the cinema buff sarcastically, 'but to whom, then, do we owe this return from the frozen north?'

'The castle has been sold and my ex-husband is in prison,' Eleanor said calmly. 'For double murder. We created our own cinema. Sebastian, I'm tired.'

Sebastian was already on his feet beside her, smiling. They thanked Mme Jedelman, a formality so rare that it only added to her stupefaction, and went out leaving a stunned silence in their wake. On the staircase to the street, Sebastian was laughing so much he could hardly get up the steps. Someone ran after them: it was the singer. He had a nice round open face.

'Can I give you a lift?' he asked.

Eleanor acquiesced, and, without so much as a glance at him, climbed into an enormous American car and gave him their address. Then Sebastian's helpless laughter communicated itself first to her, then to the singer, until they gave in to the latter's pleas to go on somewhere else to have a drink on it. He drove them home at dawn, blind drunk.

'Drive carefully,' said Eleanor amiably.

'Of course. What a marvellous evening. And what a joke, what a great joke.'

'It wasn't a joke,' Sebastian said gently. 'Good night.'

July 1971

It really is a glorious summer, this summer of 1971. It's fine and sunny; haymaking has begun. On my way here the other day, I stopped not far from Lieuray. Beneath a row of poplars. I lay down in the hay; the myriad tiny dark green leaves on the trees twisted and turned in the sunlight; I was rediscovering something. The car was parked on the side of the road like a big patient beast of burden. I had all the time in the world; I had run out of time. It wasn't at all disagreeable.

Since, fundamentally, the only idol, the only God I acknowledge is Time, it follows that I cannot experience real pleasure or pain except in relation to Time. I knew that this poplar would outlast me, that this hay, on the contrary, would wither and die before me; I knew I was expected at home and also that I could just as easily spend another hour beneath this tree. I knew that any haste on my part would be as stupid as any delay. And for the rest of my life. I knew everything. Including the fact that such knowledge meant nothing. Nothing but a privileged moment. The only authentic moments, in my view. When I say 'authentic', I mean 'instructive', which is just as silly. I shall never know enough. Never enough to be absolutely happy, never enough to have an abstract passion that will satisfy me body and soul, never enough for 'anything'. But such moments of happiness, of integration with life, if one recalls them clearly, form in the end a sort of blanket, a sort of comforting patchwork quilt with which to cover up the naked, rawboned, shivering body of our solitude.

Now it's out, the key word: solitude. That little mechanical

27

hare that is let loose on the racetrack and pursued by the frenzied, panting greyhounds of our passions, our friendships, the little hare which they never catch but which perforce they always believe to be attainable. Right up to the moment when the door of the trap is slammed in their faces. The little door in front of which they end up screeching to a halt or bashing their heads against, like Pluto. The number of Plutos there are among human beings . . .

But it's now two months since I gave a thought either to Sebastian or to Eleanor. How have they managed to eat, my poor van Milhems, what have they been living on in my absence? I feel a twinge of remorse (not too serious) in my role as guardian. I must try and remember the name of those rich people they landed up with . . . ah, yes, the Jedelmans. And I must decide whether or not in my absence Sebastian has done the necessary with that lady, not without a certain amount of grumbling, such as, 'I'm not a little gigolo any longer. After all, I'm getting on.' Here we are, nearly in August. They can't still be in the Rue de Fleurus, nor on the Côte d'Azur – that's finished. Deauville, perhaps? At all events, it would be amusing to witness the seduction scene between Mme Jedelman and Sebastian. Let's think up a *décor*: Louis XV, genuine but 'ritzy', one of those late afternoons, mild, tender, and blue, such as only Paris in summer can provide; let's have a mustard-coloured sofa and a few pieces of Knoll furniture, for 'contrast'. And let's have, with Sebastian, who needs it to give him courage, a large whisky and water. No, a neat whisky.

'Oh God,' Sebastian said under his breath, just as he had the night before, but aloud, in front of his sister. His thoughts veered from agonizing doubt as to his sexual capacities to equally agonizing certainty as to Mme Jedelman's intentions. 'Oh God, how can I get out of this? She's going to fling herself at me, she's going to drag me down into a maelstrom.' Like every child of the North, Sebastian had a superstitious horror of maelstroms.

He was stretching his long and, alas, trouser-covered legs in the Jedelmans' sumptuous drawing-room (by Boulle-Lalenne) in the Avenue Montaigne. Mme Jedelman was lying languorously on a sofa. The blond Swede had made a strong impression on her, and she had invited him round – Sebastian said 'summoned' – the very next day. There could be no question of refusal, since they were completely broke. Eleanor, compassionate and ironical, had escorted him as far as the landing like someone seeing an elder brother off to the front. And now there she was, that woman – 'la Jedelman', as she was savagely referred to in Paris. There she lay, primped, pumiced, powdered, old, admirable. No, to be fair, not old – simply no longer young. And it showed: in her neck, her armpits, her knees, her thighs, in all those cruel areas which are as revealing in a woman of a certain age as a Michelin map, every detail only too clearly marked – in short, past it.

Nora Jedelman watched with curiosity as he paced up and down. He wasn't, it was abundantly clear, what she was accustomed to: a young gigolo. No, he had a distinction of bearing, beautiful hands, a straightforward expression that intrigued her. She wondered, with a curiosity that almost equalled his, what had brought him there, first into her drawing-room, later, she hoped, into her bed. However, as he appeared to be asking himself the same question, she decided to put an end to the uncertainty even if it meant taking active measures. She rose lightly from her sofa, in a deliberately relaxed feline movement, which reminded her sharply that she was due for a visit to her osteopath next day, and glided towards Sebastian. He heard her approaching and stood frozen to the spot in front of the window, trying to call to mind some woman who had excited him, or some really effective piece of erotica. Too late. Already she was pressed against him, draped arms enfolded him, she was clasping him by the neck and the most expensive teeth New York can provide clashed with his.

To his immense surprise, he performed tolerably well, and she insisted on giving him a beautiful pair of cuff-links. These he went out and sold at once: Eleanor, his lyrebird, his sister, his accomplice, the love of his life, would be royally entertained that evening.

Chapter Five

January 1972

It's now almost six months since I abandoned this novel, my pertinent reflections, and my impertinent Swedes. Adverse circumstances, a crazy existence, idleness ... And then, last October, an autumn so lovely, so richly coloured, so heart-breaking in its splendour that from sheer happiness I won-dered how I could survive it. Alone in Normandy, exhausted but carefree, watching with amazement the rapid healing of a long laceration near my heart, watching it turn into a pink, smooth, barely perceptible scar which I would doubtless touch, later on, with an incredulous finger – the finger of memory – as though to convince myself of my own vulner-ability. And meanwhile, rediscovering the scent of grass and earth, immersing myself in it, singing *La Traviata* with reck-less abandon (you might say) at the wheel of my car, as I drove into Deauville. And in the autumnal town, deserted, blazing hot, I gazed at the empty sea, the frenzied gulls skim-ming the breakwaters, the white sun, and here and there against the light, occasional figures who might have come straight out of Visconti's *Death in Venice*. There I was, alone, finally alone, letting my hands hang down like dead birds on either side of my deck chair. Restored to solitude, to the dreams of adolescence, to everything we should never have left but which 'other people',* – hell, heaven – are for ever forcing us to abandon. But now other people were powerless to come between me and this triumphal autumn.

*

* '*L'enfer, c'est les autres,*' *Huis-clos,* Jean-Paul Sartre.

Yes, but what could my Swedes have been doing all summer? I worried about them during August in the Place de l'Atelier in Montmartre, where we were putting on a play. Local housewives, hair in curlers, bag in hand, did their daily shopping, dogs trotted happily by, transvestites sauntered in the harsh sunlight, traces of make-up still showing. Sitting on the terrace of my favourite café, I would send the van Milhems off on a cruise with the Jedelmans, or on a provincial tour with the young singer; I thought up a variety of adventures for them which I didn't write down, which I knew I would forget, for instance during the next rehearsal. Deliberately irresponsible, I didn't so much as scribble a word of it on a scrap of paper. From time to time, someone would give me a dog or a child to look after, while the owner, armed with a shopping cart, ran the gauntlet of the local supermarket. I would bandy words with a happy-go-lucky local layabout. I was happy. Later there would be the darkened auditorium, the spotlights, and the actors' problems, but for the moment the summer was gentle, Parisian, and serenely blue. I couldn't help myself. Here ends this chapter of excuses and alibis. Now I am back in Normandy. It's wet and cold; I shan't leave here until this book is finished, unless it's at gun-point. I have spoken. Amen.

'Do put that record on again,' Eleanor said.

Sebastian put out a hand and nudged the arm of the record player at his feet. He didn't need to ask which record. Having gone through a classical period, Eleanor now had a craze for a Charles Trenet record and played nothing else:

> 'On a dying branch
> The last bird of summer
> is swaying ...'

They were sitting in a swing seat on the terrace of the

Jedelman villa at Cap d'Ail. After an awkward moment or two, Sebastian had developed a certain affection for Nora Jedelman. He called her 'Lady Bird', much to her annoyance. Henry Jedelman he nicknamed 'Mr President' and, whenever he had had a bit too much to drink, would do a political assassination turn in the worst possible taste. Eleanor, having insinuated herself into the couple's affections, was once more buried in her beloved books, this time by the sea. Browned, amiable, and placid, she had watched the summer days pass as in a dream as she turned over the pages of her novels. Several of their host's smart friends had made advances to her, in vain. On the other hand, Sebastian suspected her of nocturnal assignations with the Jedelmans' gardener, an undeniably handsome young man. But he never mentioned the subject. Much as they teased one another in private about their 'romances', it was understood that their short-lived, clandestine passions should remain secret. He was well aware that it was their inviolable respect for each other's sensuality (combined with a consistent irony towards each other's emotional entanglements) that had enabled them to live together so long. By the same token, they abhorred the exhibitionism that seemed to be the rule nowadays, in this part of the world especially. They took refuge in high-necked shirts. After swimming in 1900-style bathing suits, they had scarcely dried themselves before making a dash for their clothes. They were considered bizarre and exotic, the more so since both had remarkably good figures. They thought themselves merely decent. To them, pleasure in the human body was something simple, tender, and natural, like a taste for water or a love of horses, dogs, and fire, and had nothing to do with licentiousness or aesthetics. Witness Sebastian, who took Nora Jedelman in his arms night after night without the slightest qualm, inured as he was by now to her perfume, her skin, and her somewhat querulous manner of seeking caresses. Filled with the immense tenderness of familiarity, his docile body obeyed. In any case, for them, Nordics born and bred, the sun wasn't the imperious and often sadistic god it appeared to be for others. And this, without their knowing it, increased their prestige: to turn one's back on the sun and sun-worship so unaffectedly in our time and in such a place was tantamount to turning one's back on money.

Most of the Jedelmans' friends were Americans, very rich but not yet very refined despite their constant coming and going between the United States and Europe. More often than not, it must be said, they were dependent on one another's society, most Paris salons remaining obstinately closed to them. They were sought after for charity functions and their generosity sometimes earned them an invitation to luncheon, but only at the Plaza-Athénée. Consequently, they were more than puzzled by the presence of the van Milhems, so evidently aristocratic, and by the liaison, no less evident, between Sebastian and Nora Jedelman. There was nothing of the gigolo about him (she'd had a good few of those!), and yet he and his sister were clearly living off their hosts. An old admirer of Nora's, rejected for drunkenness, ventured a remark on the subject and received a swift punch on the nose from Sebastian which put an end to the discussion. In short, they were not like other people; they were dangerous, and therefore attractive. Women far more beautiful than Nora and equally rich circled around Sebastian that summer. In vain. Well-preserved American men found themselves up against Eleanor's total indifference. Indeed, had poor Nora's tastes not been so well known and so conventional, they would have been suspected of the worst perversions.

'Tonight your faithful heart is here.
But tomorrow the swallows will be gone from the beach . . .'

Trenet was singing, the sea was turning grey. Nora appeared, wearing a mauve silk tunic which made Eleanor blink slightly.

'It's cocktail time,' she said. 'My God, that record . . . It's pretty but so sad. Especially now.'

'Turn it off,' Eleanor said to Sebastian.

She smiled sweetly at Nora, who returned her smile with a tinge of doubt. There was a great deal she would have liked to know about Eleanor, and it was no good interrogating Sebastian, who instantly shut up like a clam. All she knew was that wherever Eleanor was, Sebastian was bound to be. And if this was reassuring in one sense, it was a trifle vexing in another. She had even pushed Dave Burby, a magnificent catch and a charming fellow, into Eleanor's arms. Without success. And who was this Hugo who was in prison in Sweden? And whence had she herself acquired this mysterious and courteous lover who accepted her presents with absent-minded politeness and who, at the age of forty, had fits of uncontrollable laughter and the inexplicable moods of a youth? She was growing fond of him, in spite of her profound cynicism – she had always known how to buy and what she was buying. That was what worried her. What did he intend to do in Paris? Where did he intend to live with his dreamy sister? Was he counting on her or on luck? He never spoke to her about going back, and yet they were all due to leave in three days' time.

Mario the gardener was coming up the path with an armful of gaudy dahlias which he held out to Nora with a smile. Eleanor gazed at him tenderly. When she had opened her bedroom window on their first morning there, she had seen that slim, bronzed back, the deft movements of those long arms as he pruned a tree, the brown neck. When he turned around, he had smiled at her politely at first, then stopped smiling. Whereupon *she* had smiled at him before closing her window. When the household was sleeping or on those evenings when everyone went to Monte Carlo or Cannes, she would go and meet him at the bottom of the garden. There was the tool shed, which smelt of fresh mint and pine needles, there were the local village hops where he would take her dancing, there was Mario's delighted laugh, Mario's fresh mouth, Mario's glowing body, a body which had no need of massage. He was unspoiled, tender, and carefree, and she could relax in his company, away from that over-furnished house, those loud-mouthed people, the clinking of dollars. Sebastian had taken the responsibility for their holiday, after all. Sebastian, the ideal brother.

'Give those dahlias to Madame van Milhem,' said Nora. 'Aren't they beautiful? That mauve . . .'

Mario turned towards Eleanor and handed her the bouquet. His shirt fell open and she saw, on his neck, the purple mark left by her own teeth two nights before, the same colour as the open blooms. She touched his hand accidentally and he smiled at her. And Sebastian, amazed, saw the reflection of a thousand memories and regrets mingle with the setting sun in his sister's pale eyes.

Yes, I know: I've relapsed into my old frivolous ways. That famous little Saganesque world where real problems don't exist. Well, it's true. The reason is that I too am getting fed up, in spite of my infinite patience. After having stated and believed (which I still do) that a capable woman should be paid as much as a capable man; after having stated that women should be free to choose whether or not to have a baby, and that abortion should be legalized, since otherwise it's a mere nuisance for women with means and a sinister butchery for the rest; after having sworn by all I hold sacred that I myself had had an abortion, and having read in a weekly magazine that the whole thing could be summed up in the slogan, 'Women, your womb is yours and yours alone' (how sad, for one thing, but above all what a phrase!); after having signed a multitude of petitions; after having listened to the woes of bankers, grocers, taxi drivers, all apparently on the brink of ruin, and having myself been literally stripped of all I possess by a tax collector turned raving lunatic (one should've been wary of Giscard d'Estaing from the outset: I never trusted those polo-necks of his. Where are they now, by the way?); after having nearly smashed fifteen television sets from sheer nausea and nearly fallen out of my theatre seat from boredom during ten 'popular' shows; after having witnessed the apathy of some, the impotent rage of others, the good will, bad faith, and chaos which prevail in this smug Louis-Phillippard régime; after having seen old-age pensioners shivering with cold, standing in line for their blue 'benefit' cards; after having listened to extremist speeches, moderate speeches, stupid speeches, intelligent speeches; after having found myself – in spite of my dashing sports car – back among the have-nots; after all that, dear reader, I'm going to escape this instant to an imaginary dream-world 'where money doesn't count'. That's that. It's my right, after all, just as it's the right of every citizen not to buy my complete works. This age often exasperates me, I confess. I'm not a glutton for work, and conscientiousness isn't my strong point. But now, thanks to literature, I'm going to enjoy myself with my friends the van Milhems. I have spoken. Amen.

Chapter Six

Without being in the least sadistic, Nora Jedelman enjoyed making her power felt. So she waited until they were in her Cadillac between Orly and Paris before asking Sebastian and Eleanor where she could drop them.

'Eight, Rue Madame,' Sebastian said airily. 'If it's not out of your way.'

She felt snubbed. She was hoping to hear either 'at the Crillon', meaning he was cornered, or 'wherever you suggest', meaning he trusted her. She had held her tongue for ten whole days, all to no purpose. She was at a loss.

'Do you have friends there?'

'We don't live only with friends,' said Sebastian with an easy, friendly laugh. 'Someone we know has found us a two-room flat. Very attractive, I gather, and the rent's reasonable.'

You'll only have to sell your Cartier watch or your cigarette case, thought Nora crossly. In fact, she had decided in her own mind to put Eleanor in the spare room for the time being, while Sebastian could have the study next to her own room. She had visualized herself as a cross between a Lady Bountiful and a fairy godmother come to the rescue. This unexpected initiative deprived her not only of her role but of Sebastian's familiar, lazy presence. Now she would be returning to her immense flat alone – her husband was still in New York – except for her chihuahuas. Panic gripped her.

'It's ridiculous,' she said, 'I could easily have put you up.'

'You've put up with us quite enough,' said Eleanor calmly, 'all this summer. We don't want to impose.'

She's making fun of Nora, thought Sebastian, amused. *I must say it's justified, for once. What's the idea of leaving people in the air like that? When I think what I've gone through to raise money in three days, selling all those cuff links and expressing money orders to poor old Robert. Especially when I loathe haggling and lining up at post offices. It's lucky that Robert knows this part of Paris so well. I hope it'll be liveable in. Oh well, for three months . . .* He had had to pay three months' rent in advance.

The car stopped in front of an old apartment building. Nora seemed momentarily shattered.

'We'll telephone you very soon,' Eleanor said politely.

They were both standing on the pavement, holding their suitcases, not even knowing how to get in, but slim, blond, and unconcerned. *Payable but not buyable,* thought Nora despairingly. And in any event, together. Not alone. She braced herself, gave them a wave, and fell back in her seat. The Cadillac drove off. Brother and sister smiled at one another.

'I'm glad about one thing,' said Eleanor, 'it's on the ground floor. Where's the concierge?'

The flat was gloomy in the extreme, giving on to an exiguous garden, no more than a strip of grass. A bare room separated to bedrooms, minuscule and silent. There was a red divan and a bottle of whisky on the only table, with a note from Robert, the faithful Robert, welcoming them.

'What do you think of it?' asked the concierge. 'It's a bit dark in summer, but in winter . . .'

'It's fine,' said Eleanor, stretching out on the divan. 'Thanks a lot. Where did I put my book?'

And, to the astonishment of the concierge, she rummaged in a large handbag and went back to the thriller she had started on the aeroplane. The suitcases lay in a jumble on the floor and Sebastian prowled like a cat through the three rooms.

'It's perfect,' he said at last. 'Perfect. By the way, Madame' (addressing the concierge), 'I can't help admiring your make-up.'

'Quite right,' said Eleanor, looking up. 'I noticed it to. It's most unusual and attractive.'

The concierge backed out, all smiles. It was true, she took a lot of trouble with her appearance; this M. van Milhem had something. His sister too, come to that. Out of the top drawer, you could tell from their manner (and their luggage). A little vague, perhaps. They wouldn't stay long, she supposed, and already, obscurely, she was missing them.

'I must telephone Nora,' said Sebastian. 'She hasn't got our number, after all, and it was unkind to abandon her alone in that Cadillac, like a suitcase.'

'Ah, but a Vuitton suitcase,' said Eleanor, still engrossed in her novel. It was plain to see that she had found the perfect refuge in that worn, shapeless, and rather grubby divan.

She had placed her cigarettes and matches within reach, and taken off her shoes. Her thriller, even if it was a bit too sordid and full of detectives who were a bit too squeamish, certainly wasn't boring. Sebastian, meanwhile, paced up and down. Now that the novelty had worn off, the flat appeared ludicrously small, squalid, and quite incompatible with the sort of lives they led. Sebastian was beginning to show symptoms of what the Germans call *Katzenjammer*. For once, his sister's air of nonchalant calm filled him with a sort of nervous irritability, something that rarely happened to him, a condition which owed more to inaction (he didn't know what to do with himself from one moment to the next) than to the uncertainty of their general situation. He had no inclination to unpack, search for coat-hangers, put things away. Nor did he have any desire to go to some café or other, although as a rule cafés were his favourite haunts. The fact was that he didn't want to be left alone – for he suddenly felt very much alone in the face of Eleanor's exaggerated impassivity as she read her detective story. He felt she ought to 'do something' (the words were in quotes in his head) and realized belatedly that this 'something' had been done for the past two or three months – thanks to the physical attraction he exercised over her and thanks to her money – by Nora Jedelman. He felt adolescent, sulky, ignored, and considered that Eleanor – who hadn't put herself out by one iota all summer – might at the very least show some awareness of it. In short, he felt like Chéri without Lea, and a forty-year-old Chéri at that; his demoralization was complete.

'Why a Vuitton?' he asked aggressively.

'They're the most solid,' replied Eleanor, still without looking at him. And at the thought of the undoubted solidity, comfort, and organization of the Jedelmans, Sebastian felt a nostalgia that was literally physical.

Sebastian van Milhem was, in a way, like old Karamazov. He found something to appeal to him in all women. And certain women he had even preferred for their physical defects rather than their qualities. As long as they never talked to him about such things, either gaily or sadly, he had never been repelled by over-developed hips, a scrawny neck, or a wrinkled hand. For him, love, dark love, had nothing to do with Miss France but a great deal to do with Gilles de Rais, Henry VIII, Baudelaire and his heavy mulatto mistress. He knew that many a man – often a man of genius – has been captivated by one of those large ill-favoured women solely because of her exultant acceptance of her own body as of a friend, an animal dedicated as much to her pleasure as to the man's, a body, in a word, in love with love. And warm. It was all men wished for: to lose themselves, having aroused it, in someone else's pleasure, to be both master and servant, whipper and whipped.

Sebastian had always been susceptible to all this, and now that he had established a sexual relationship with this woman who was older than himself and less attractive as a woman than he as a man, he realized that her admiration for him had become something more than a physical stimulant. What he felt was a sort of pride, generous and unashamed, which he might have translated *à la Clovis*: 'Bow your head, proud Sebastian, worship her who worships you – and content yourself with that, for it can sometimes suffice.'*

'What do you mean, "the most solid"?'

Eleanor turned towards him, put her novel down in her lap, and burst out laughing.

'Stop acting the gentleman, darling. I didn't mean Nora's money or even her body. I was thinking of her genuine affection for you. And I agree that you ought to telephone her, she's probably lonely and scared. If I were you, I'd be off to her like a shot, and tomorrow when you come back you'll find a ravishing house, all fixed up by the elves and fairies – in other words, me.'

They looked at one another warily, like a couple of Siamese cats suddenly hesitant or at cross purposes at the sight of a mouse. There was no sign either of contempt or pity between them, merely, for once, no complicity.

An hour later, in the taxi taking him to the Avenue Montaigne where a delighted Nora awaited him, Sebastian thought to himself that the reprobate, the gypsy, the Van Gogh of the partnership was no longer he but Eleanor, who, in some way, and he didn't know where or when, had thrown down her weapons.

* *'Courbe la tête, fier Sicambre, adore ce que tu as brûlé, brûle ce que tu as adoré.'* Baptism of King Clovis I at Reims in 496.

Chapter Seven

February 1972

I swore that I wouldn't leave here (my country retreat) except at gun-point and with my finished manuscript under my arm. But alas, the fates are against me. There's an astral phenomenon hovering over the van Milhems and myself at present, as a result of which, having plunged several feet off the road, here I am in Paris, broken-boned and X-rayed. Nothing serious, I need hardly say. I really don't believe – and I trust my faithful readers are touching wood – I really don't believe the vehicle exists, however high-powered, horse-powered, or even horse-drawn, that could destroy me. Only my moral arguments and my good resolutions are destructible. Such as: 'I'm off to the country, I'm going to work, I've had enough fun and games, it's time I wrote something worthwhile.' Close quotes.

Now I come to think of it, there have been a lot of quotation marks in my life, as well as a few exclamation marks (passion), question marks (nervous depression), suspension mark (indifference) and, having got that far along the road to the full stop that was due to be placed solemnly at the end of my manuscript (awaited with flattering impatience by my publisher), here I am held up by yet more punctuation marks – stitches – strapped, swaddled (at my age!) in elastic bandages that I could well have done without. Or could I? As long as my indifference (suspension marks) doesn't reassert itself and, taking advantage of this ideal alibi – my accident – I don't relapse into that happy state of non-being which consists of gazing out of the window, with a sort of mindless, motionless ferocity, at the trees in the Luxembourg Gardens. And which also consists nowadays of refusing systematically every reception, every first night, every place to which I'm invited *qua* Sagan, 'La Sagan' as they say in Italy. Refusals that are not in the least calculated but simply a reflection of my tendency to giggle nervously at the mere thought of the image people still have of me. Not that this image hasn't had its uses, but I've nevertheless spent the best part of eighteen years hidden behind a screen of Ferraris, bottles of whisky, gossip, marriages, divorces, in short, what the public thinks of as the artist's life. However, I ought to be grateful for this delightful mask which, however rudimentary, does reflect undeniable tastes of mine: speed, the sea, midnight, brilliance, blackness, risk and thus self-discovery. For nothing will alter my conviction that only by pursuing the extremes in one's nature, with all its contradictions, appetites, aversions, rages, can one hope to understand a little – oh, I admit only a very little – of what life is about. At any rate, my life.

I might add, and here I put on a moral veil (it's a great pity that veils have disappeared, they were most becoming), I might add that if it came to the crunch, I would still be prepared to die for certain moral and aesthetic principles, but I have no wish to shout my beliefs from the rooftops. It only needs someone, some day, to attack them to my face for it to be quite clear what they are. Besides, it's a well-known fact that my signature at the bottom of a manifesto makes a rather frivolous impression. People have often reproached me for it in the very same breath as they ask for my signature, which I've never given except for serious reasons. I haven't often been taken seriously and it's understandable; but it should be realized that it was difficult in 1954 (my hour of glory) for me to choose between the two roles offered to me: scandalous writer or conventional young girl. I was, after all, neither. In fact, I would have found it easier to be a scandalous young girl or a conventional writer. I certainly wasn't going to choose between two equally false propositions for the sake of people whom in any case I didn't respect. My only option, and I'm deeply thankful for it, was to do what I wanted to do: have my fling. And a fine fling I've had, what's more, in between writing various novels and various plays. And that's my story in a nutshell. What else was I to do, after all? I've always been tempted to burn the candle at both ends, drink, play the fool. And what if I enjoy this absurd and frivolous game in our petty, sordid, and cruel age which nevertheless, by some extraordinary stroke of luck for which I am duly grateful, has also provided me with the means of escaping it. Ah, ah!

And what about you, dear readers, what are your lives like? Does your mother love you? And your father? Was he an example to you, or a nightmare? Whom did you love before life caught you in its trap? And has anyone yet told you what colour your eyes really are, or your hair? And are you scared at night? And do you dream aloud? And if you're a man, are you a prey to those terrible fits of gloom that horrify insensitive women, those who don't understand – and are proud of it, to make matters worse – that every woman should hold a man beneath her wing, in the warm, whenever she can, and look after him? Do you realize that everyone, from your boss to your concierge, or that horrible traffic cop in the street, or, come to that, poor old Mao, who's responsible for an entire nation, do you realize that each and every one of them feels himself alone and is almost as afraid of life as he is of death – just like you, in fact? Such commonplaces are frightening only because they are always forgotten in so-called human relationships. People want to win, or simply to survive.

Just look at yourselves, little Frenchmen, well-fed, ill-mannered, showing off wherever you are – even to your partner in the act of love. Conformism and snobbery lurk under the bedclothes with the same arrogant complacency as in drawing-rooms. No one, but no one, ever behaves 'well' in bed unless they love or are loved – two conditions seldom fulfilled. And sometimes – horror of horrors! – it's as though no one loved anyone. As though the whole tense, incoherent, inevitable, almost cruel dialogue we have, or try to have, with one another had suddenly become a sort of iron curtain. Speaking as someone who is always trying vaguely but doggedly to understand and who has remained on good terms with life, it sometimes seems as though I can't go on any longer, as though my interlocutors can't go on any longer. And I want to shake the dust from my sandals and flee to India. (Though I doubt whether the hippy trail would be exactly suitable for a Maserati.) And yet the people I talk to and who talk to me are my friends, and we understand each other. But in the end I think of us as being like those soldiers clad in iron and steel on the strange vessels invented by Fellini in *Satyricon*, who are being carried towards the beach where Tiberius is to die. Except that those boats, as Fellini himself told me, were imaginary. They could never have floated, and the first warrior to lose his balance would have sunk without trace if Fellini hadn't kept an eye on them. But God is not Fellini, and one day we shall all find ourselves out of our depth without having understood very much. But with a little luck, we shall find a hand, iron-gloved or not, gripping our own.

Chapter Eight

Having finished her thriller, which ended as badly as a thriller possibly can – the guilty killed, the innocent wounded, and the detectives more and more disillusioned – Eleanor examined with a sort of wry amusement the dark red walls, the Louis-Philippe table with the three knick-knacks perched on top of it, that were henceforth to be her constant companions. Sebastian had fled, a very rare occurrence. She could perfectly well understand him. For her, every action, every love affair, every relationship was a sort of compromise: you won, you lost, or, in Sebastian's case, you got the jitters. After taking a few vague and listless steps around the empty flat, she ended up by finding a mirror and gazing at herself in it. Clearly she must renew her make-up, put on mascara and lipstick and thus, by artificial means, revivify the one reality she still felt certain of, her body. She no longer wanted anything. She was no longer afraid of anything. 'As for living,' to quote Villiers de l'Isle-Adam, 'our servants will do that for us.' There was something so absurd in the grimaces she made in blacking the lashes of those eyes that had really seen far too much, in renewing the shape of that mouth that had known far too many other mouths, something so preposterous in her combing and shaping that hair which had invariably been destined to be disarranged by other hands, impatient, virile hands which had never under any circumstances gone so far or, more precisely, so high as to reach the rachidian bulb deep in the nape of the neck which, we are told, is the centre, the great reasoner, the

47

chairman and managing director of all the sensations.

Eleanor had neither the strength nor the desire to unpack. Paris seemed to her as lustreless as a dimmed light bulb, and this almost unbearably gloomy flat, instead of making things worse, in fact accorded with a state of mind which she scarcely even needed to formulate: *'Well, there we are, at least summer's over and done with.'* Having made herself up to look a stranger to herself, to her brother, to anyone, knowing that she was incapable of going out in the circumstances she had created for herself, knowing that she was incapable of doing anything, except perhaps reading another thriller – but this would have to be bought, and she was incapable of crossing the threshold – she lay down again on the decrepit sofa, fully made up and incidentally very beautiful, and waited. She waited first of all for her heart to calm down, for the crazy imbecile which had never beaten faster for anyone – and a part of her had often reproached it for that – was now beating like an overwound clock, too regular, too insistent, and so loud that her temples were throbbing. There was literally nothing she could do. She couldn't talk to the concierge, nice though she found her. She couldn't point out to Sebastian the absurdity of his behaviour because she was, after all, the cause of it. She couldn't go and visit Hugo because the walls of Stockholm prison were too thick. She couldn't go back to Mario (shades of summer), who would certainly have forgotten her just as she had forgotten him. There had always been, in the background of her life, a kind of deathly sadness, a resigned loneliness against which she had fought for ten years, roughly between the ages of eighteen and twenty-eight; and now that it was completely ineradicable, she felt it welling up, more powerful, uglier, intensified in this dark and squalid flat where even her brother, her Castor, her Pollux, had abandoned her. She thought briefly of some white pills which she knew to be quick-acting, but dismissing this as a little too vulgar, a little too obvious to be exact, she took herself to bed in one of the two beds obligingly made up by the concierge. If, in her sleep, she embraced the pillow as though it were a child or a man, it was really because sleep overcame her natural impulses.

If there's a tiresome side to this delightful profession – vocation – need – mental suicide – compensation – it is that after eighteen years, which has been my stint, one has suffered, in the true sense of the word, every conceivable type of remark. For instance, I've always been blessed with jolly ladies or earnest young people who tell me how much they've enjoyed (a) *Bonjour Tristesse* and (b) of my plays, *Château en Suède*. However well-intentioned, this is mildly depressing for an author, because you have the impression of having produced two beautiful healthy children who have done well for themselves and, thereafter, a succession of little lame ducks which, poor things, have been less presentable. This category of readers is the most usual. Next, there are those who have 'seen' one's books: 'I enjoyed *Bonjour Tristesse* as much as everyone else, but actually my special weakness is for *Aimez-vous Brahms*. Goodness, wasn't Ingrid Bergman marvellous in that!' The third category is more subtle: 'Technically, you know, that play was badly produced.' (Here I blush with shame since I produced it myself.) 'But I think of all your plays my favourite is *Bonheur, Impair et Passe.*' The fourth category is more specialized still and thus even more unorthodox: 'As a matter of fact, the only book of yours I've liked' (the implication being that the rest belonged in the wastepaper basket), 'the only one that has something violent, obsessional about it, is *Les Merveilleux Nuages.*' One's resulting behaviour is altogether peculiar, a mixture of the mother hen ready to defend her chicks against unwarranted attacks and of resigned acquiescence – it all depends on the day and the looks of the

49

speaker – which can lead you to fly at someone's throat thinking, *You poor fool, that's my best book!* Without in fact knowing which. Or alternatively, *How right you are, the whole thing's not worth the paper it's written on.*

This mixture of ingenuousness, offensiveness, and politeness with which people talk to you about your work is pretty staggering, when you come to think of it. Nevertheless, it's perfectly logical: you present them with two or three hundred pages of prose – in my case more like two hundred – for which they pay fifteen or twenty francs, or twenty-five for a seat in the theatre, and they feel they have the right, if not the duty, to inform you of their reactions. I even wonder whether some of them don't believe they're doing you a favour. What they never think of adding to the price of the book is the sort of colossal VAT – mental, moral, psychological, morbid, unendurable – represented by the silence that sometimes reigns between someone who likes writing and the blank sheet of paper in front of him. Not to mention the countless dodges to avoid seeing the desk at which one should be sitting, and the countless dodges to avoid seeing the sun or the rain outside, both terrible temptations. I've always had the greatest admiration for those people – and there seem to be a great many – who write in cafés. I suspect that in a café I'd spend my time watching the faces of the other customers, chatting with the waiter, making eyes, or trying to, at some handsome Latin American. The least thing distracts me once I'm no longer alone. Let there be anything amusing, anything distressing, and it monopolizes my attention. I need to be locked in with a double lock by an inflexible hand – a hand that has to be mine, alas, and God knows my hands don't lack flexibility – before I can get down to work. Once or twice in my life I've tried to get other people to lock me in, kind souls who were concerned about me and had little faith in my will power, but then my defunct will power sprang up like a flea, and I was prepared to scale balconies, slide down drainpipes, scream the place down until I was let out. Screaming, of course, that literature was a matter of inspiration, that I refused to be a bureaucrat, that I wasn't being paid piece rates, that I was no longer a twelve-year-old, etc., etc.

It's a strange life, the writer's. He has to keep himself on a tight rein, to a well-regulated pace, his backbone rigid, when ideally he should be like a runaway horse, mane flying in the wind, leaping with the greatest of ease such ridiculous obstacles as grammar, syntax, or laziness, the latter being a gigantic fence. When I think that this profession is called a liberal profession, when I think that you don't even have a boss to rap you over the knuckles, that there's no one, literally no one, to correct our copy, and when I think that freedom, in the last analysis, is only what you can grab and that the only person you can grab it from in this case is yourself – burglar burgled, biter bit, that's our lot; we're our own worst tormentors – when I think of my miserable fate, which consists of doing what I want when I want and, what's more, being extremely well paid for it, I feel like bursting into tears. Anyway, I hope that my readers and my publishers will understand what I mean and will have enough imagination to feel sorry for me.

In that case, I can hear you saying, why write at all? In the first place, for ignoble reasons: because I'm an old campaigner and if I don't write for two or three years I feel like a half-wit. Alas! No sooner are my books published than a certain section of the critics treats me exactly as though I *were* a half-wit. By nature easily swayed, I stop writing, not without a feeling of considerable relief. Then, two years later, the echo of those beloved voices (the critics) having died away, my own judgement reasserts itself: *'My poor dear, you're nothing but a half-wit.'* You see what a delightful vicious circle it is, what fun it is to be a 'successful writer' in Paris in 1972. Wait, I still haven't finished complaining! This life of honey and roses, of indulgence, gaiety, and folly – you must be able to endure it! You need a will of iron to resist the boredom, the obligations, the conventions, in short everything that goes to make up, on whatever social level, the rallying points for all and sundry. You need to be very well-balanced if you're to roam freely, wherever you like, without this becoming for you yourself no more than a delicious busman's holiday.

Chapter Nine

Sebastian lay on his back between the deliciously soft sheets (from Porthault's) of Nora Jedelman's bed. It was a warm night and the footsteps and voices of late passers-by in the Avenue Montaigne could be heard through the open window. Everything had been comforting at first: Nora's welcome, for once almost shy, no doubt from relief; the internal but endearing yaps of the chihuahuas; and, above all, the vast expanse of beige carpet recalling the sea he had just left, and as reassuring. Then a somewhat premature log fire, several whiskies, with ice this time, and finally, of course, someone who needed him, loved him, and told him so. But now he felt a deserter. The heavily beringed hand resting on his shoulder seemed to grow heavier and heavier, while the voice, slightly nasal even when whispering, became more and more penetrating.

'Poor Eleanor,' the voice said, and the word 'poor' immediately put Sebastian's back up. 'You've left her all alone.'

'My sister adores being alone,' Sebastian replied. 'As you should know.'

'Your sister's odd,' the voice said. 'I used to wonder ... you know, when I introduced her to that charming Dave Burby, she didn't so much as look at him. She was happier talking to the girl he brought with him, Candice.'

'Really?' murmured Sebastian absently.

'I even wondered for a moment' (there was an embarrassed giggle in the darkness) 'whether your sister mightn't prefer women.'

Sebastian yawned and turned on his side.

'If that Candice girl attracted her – and I must say I found her much more amusing than Burby – Eleanor wouldn't have hesitated for a moment,' he said.

'My God,' wailed Nora, whose Protestant sentiments were occasionally aroused, especially after making love.

'Don't worry,' Sebastian went on, 'Eleanor slept with the gardener all summer.'

'My God,' exclaimed Nora, whose snobbery was even more acute than her conventionality, 'with Mario?'

'Yes, with Mario,' said Sebastian. 'As a matter of fact, apart from me he was the best-looking man around.'

There was a moment's icy silence, highly agreeable to Sebastian, who was growing allergic to the sheets, the chihuahuas huddled beneath the dressing table, and this woman with her never-ending questions. The silence was less agreeable to Nora, who, like many people from a relatively modest background who have acquired a certain degree of wealth together with what they called in their horrible jargon a certain 'status', considered a liaison with a servant the height of depravity. Although all such women have a tendency (indeed a conscious desire) to turn their lovers into valets, the opposite would seem to them unthinkable. All things considered, she would have preferred Eleanor to have had a dubious liaison with the Candice girl, who was at least the daughter of a well-known Dallas textile manufacturer. There could obviously be no question of her condemning Eleanor's behaviour to Sebastian's face; she was well aware that that would automatically result in his leaving her for good. But as mistress of the house, it was her duty to stigmatize such goings-on and make her disapproval felt, tactfully of course, to Sebastian. Besides, the poor darling no doubt went through agonies because of his sister's penchant for servants. Like all slightly dimwitted people, she instantly confused an isolated incident with a long-standing vice.

Consequently, she visualized Sebastian dragging his sister from hotel to hotel, avoiding good-looking barmen, dodging dubious waiters, in constant despair at Eleanor's lack of 'breeding'. The cynicism he affected was surely no more than a front he put on for his sister's sake. Gorged, overwhelmed with noble sentiments, her eyes almost brimming with tears, she put her head on his shoulder and squeezed his hand eloquently. At this, Sebastian felt the laughter welling up inside him. He had said what he'd said without thinking, for a laugh, as usual, and also because it was true; but the last thing he expected his harmless tale to produce (God knows, they had heard worse, Eleanor and he) was such a virginal reaction. That of a Latin or Nordic woman would have been infinitely preferable, someone who said gaily, 'But of course, Mario. What a fool I am, I'd never have thought it.' Instead, all America lay there beside him, and even though the sheets were Porthault sheets the *Mayflower* was sailing alongside, and with it Quakerism, money, what's done and what isn't done, the Bible, and far and away the most important, the comments of her girl-friends. Between these soft European sheets, these famous sheets covered with pale-tinted flowers, European flowers, a fierce wind blew that came from the prairies, the American Constitution, the Far West, and the banks of Boston. He was delighted at the indignation he sensed in the small, plump, comfortable body beside him, the little body that owed its enjoyment far more to Bostonian dollars than to the precepts of the Bible. Suddenly, as he was choking back the first spasm of laughter, he thought of Eleanor in the sordid furnished flat where he had abandoned her, thought of her long and slender form, her hands lying open – she always slept with her hands open – thought of her rather too elongated eyelids closed over her grey eyes, grey like his own, thought of her utter lack of vulgarity or calculation; and, not for the first time, the realization that they were of the same blood and, if not twins, forever condemned to the same reflexes, the same scruples, stabbed him to the quick, frightening him. '*This time,*' he told himself, now sitting on the bed, his eyes still shining with tears of laughter (at the mere thought of the *Mayflower*), '*I really will be degrading myself if I stay here,*' and, still laughing, he got up and dressed, in spite of poor Nora's tearful questions and avowals of love. Unable to utter a word, unable even to explain that he had come with the best intentions in the world and that pity for her loneliness in this oversized flat had counted for as much as his own restlessness in his decision to come; unable, therefore, to reassure her, he went down the stairs four at a time, still roaring with laughter, and emerged into the cold early morning air of the Avenue Montaigne, where he began running in the direction of the Rue Madame – at least for the short time it took him to find a taxi. No sooner had he arrived than he woke Eleanor up by tripping over his suitcase in the hall, and she sat up in bed and murmured, 'Oh, it's you,' with an air of amiable surprise, as though she had been expecting someone else. Then he sat on her bed and told her everything and they laughed so much all night, with fifty cigarette stubs in each ashtray marked 'Martini', and a bottle that they constantly passed back and forth – they laughed so much that at noon on the following day they were still asleep, exhausted, happy, together again.

Chapter Ten

What I find agreeable about this novel that I'm writing from day to day, and what I sincerely hope, is that this time no one, really no one, will come to me and say, 'You know, it's a funny thing, but Sebastian is so like me,' or 'Eleanor is absolutely me'. (I'm less worried about Nora Jedelman.) Nothing is more tedious than this process of identification that seems, alas, to be at the root of literary success, at any rate of mine. I've had the most monstrous women explain to me how much of themselves they recognized in Paule in *Aimez-vous Brahms,* or whatever; I've known strange people, utterly remote from my imagining, who, in their own, closely correspond to my heroes. But I can't believe that anyone is going to see his or her alter ego in one of these two crazy Swedes. Perhaps a few licentious spirits will tell me that they too know all about incest. But otherwise? It seems to me hard to identify oneself with characters like these.

Nevertheless, when the monstrous women in question murmured, 'You know, that happened to me,' I was sure that in a way it was true. It isn't common sense that is paramount in this world, it's wishful thinking. And the plain woman who imagines herself having to choose between a steady middle-aged man and an over-eager lover isn't making it up: at some time or other she has had occasion to believe it, or at least the burning desire to do so; and in the last analysis our fantasy life bears a close resemblance to, in fact is almost indistinguishable from, the life we actually live. Inasmuch as the most precious ingredient – the gold, the salt, the very water – to be found in this repast, this strange repast which is known as conversation between two human beings, inasmuch as this ingredient is imagination, and is exceedingly rare, and is the only thing that people need, desire, and sometimes possess, but can never command; this thing called imagination, which is justly known as the mad boarder in the house of the mind, which alone can prevent a house from being built on safe, practical, and boring foundations – in short, to end my sentence, we would do well to realize that it is the only thing that counts. What I'm trying to say is that if we don't use a little imagination in our relations with our friends, we may find that they have killed themselves stupidly for the simple reason that, one night, we were lacking in imagination where they were concerned. By the same token, it may happen that we ourselves, alone and in utter despair for one reason or another, suddenly feel a glow of warmth and the will to live simply because some minor occurrence or other awoke the poor mad creature. It may happen, if one is engaged in so-called creative work, that one finds oneself chasing the mad boarder for nights on end, half bewitched, half terrified, like children chasing bats in country houses in summer. It may happen that one has the impression, on meeting a person, of being confronted with someone maimed, almost totally disfigured – regardless of his or her intrinsic beauty – simply and solely because the mad boarder has never been under their roof. It may happen that one falls in love with a frantic liar because, trapped between two lies and cornered (squeezed, to use an expression from bridge) in front of witnesses, he gets out of it with a third lie that puts him in an admirable light. God knows I've met plenty of mythomaniacs, as they are contemptuously called nowadays, in my life. I'm not speaking of defensive mythomania, which is always rather depressing; I'm speaking of the other sort, which is designed to please. I've been its happy victim for a very long time and have learned to detect it by purely physical signs, of which I ought to draw up a list for the readers of women's magazines, as follows: an air of calm, a rather monotonous voice, a way of looking you straight in the eye with more than usual gravity and, *pace* all those Provençal films, an absence of exaggerated gestures. Mythomaniacs hold a very special charm for me; more often than not they lie gratuitously; you could almost say that they lie as much to please you as to please themselves. There is the masochistic mythomaniac (rare, alas) who tells stories against himself, and that is the primary form of humour; then there is the paranoid mythomaniac (the most common, alas) who joyfully recounts his triumphs, his successes, his glorious moments. I cannot and would not for the world interrupt either – unless they were deadly bores. (There is also, tragically, the mythomaniac without imagination, the obsessive mythomaniac, the kind who scatters all the night owls, as a scarecrow scatters birds, the moment he enters a night-club or a bar.) I have two reasons for not wanting to interrupt them: first, because they're trying to change their lives by reconstructing them – and what else is literature, after all? – and second, because it's out of a desire to please that they seek to lead us through their hoops. If only sceptics would understand that some of the lies they are told, and especially some of the tall stories, are a kind of tribute to themselves: they're being credited with enough intelligence to grasp the basic premise, enough imagination to hope for a dénouement, enough childishness to suppose that there is one, and enough sensitivity not to say, 'Stop talking such rubbish.' People whose lives have been enriched by such far-fetched, bizarre fabrications, and who complain about them, should realize that they have been nourished and refreshed thereby, and that through them, for once and for nothing, the imperious, loving, glowing hand of the mad boarder has been laid on their forehead.

*

Mme Schiller, the concierge, had brought them some strong black coffee to wake them up and made a timely offer to unpack for them. She found it really rather shocking that this Mme van Milhem's lovely outfits should still be lying crushed together at the bottom of a suitcase after twenty-four hours. And this natural sense of outrage in a woman who knew how to make the best of herself (as we have seen) and consequently had a respect for elegance, was beginning to be reinforced by the slightly anxious solicitude, the spontaneous devotion that the van Milhems always managed to arouse whenever they chanced to be travelling on their own. Already she had taken in hand the problems of heating, coal, electricity, and other public corporations, secretly delighted with these two belated children who had suddenly fallen into her arms (M. Schiller had never wanted children). In language that was flowery but effective, she held forth on the telephone while brother and sister nonchalantly munched their toast. The presence of Mme Schiller in their life, and in the organization of it, seemed to them as natural – dreadful though it is to say – as that of Nora Jedelman. Indeed, they found her less obtrusive and, to Eleanor's eyes, far better made up.

'Poor old Nora,' said Sebastian, 'if she wants to ring up, she'll never get through. Our flat's a regular quartermaster-general's office.'

'While she showered you with ravishing trinkets, you gave her a poisoned gift,' Eleanor said. 'That was unkind.'

'What gift?' Sebastian asked.

'You gave her back the taste for love,' said Eleanor, stretching her limbs and going into the bathroom (or what passed for one), only to re-emerge and tell Mme Schiller that there was no hot water.

It so happened that Mme Schiller's best friend was the wife of the plumber (an elusive fellow) and she revelled in the chance to show off about it.

'I've got about four thousand francs left,' said Sebastian. 'The rent's paid for three months, but we've got to feed and clothe ourselves.'

'Oh, clothes,' said Eleanor, 'when one's as brown as we are . . .'

'All the same, it's a bit inadequate as a substitute,' said Sebastian. 'No, I'll get a job.'

Eleanor's outburst of laughter almost sabotaged the delicate negotiations between Mme Schiller and the plumber's wife. Eleanor seldom laughed aloud, but when she did, it was with a low, irresistible, contagious laugh, what her brother called 'a Garbo laugh'. Sebastian was annoyed.

'When you've quite calmed down, I'll telephone Robert. Or else, if you'd prefer, we can buy three thousand francs' worth of whisky and polish it off here and now. With any luck it might be the death of us.'

'I doubt it, with our constitutions,' replied Eleanor. 'Why don't you ask Mme Schiller? She'll find you a job as a keeper in the Luxembourg Gardens.'

'I'm sure she could, but that's against my principles. Can you see me chasing after lovers and children, turning away dogs, and blowing my whistle like a madman at five o'clock? No thanks!'

'I wouldn't mind doing dressmaking by the day,' said Eleanor suddenly. 'I'd stay here, and I'd sew with one hand and read with the other.'

'Unfortunately, you can't sew, and anyhow I think you need two hands,' said Sebastian.

They sat there, blissfully absorbed. They loved solemnly exchanging ideas for impracticable and humble jobs, and had they been capable of doing them, no doubt such relatively independent occupations would have been morally more acceptable than being kept by others. (Morally in the sense of morale, not morality.)

'I've got the plumber,' cried Mme Schiller. 'I caught him on the wing and he'll be with us this evening.'

The 'us' made them smile: they had managed to acquire a mother. Carried away by her enthusiasm, Sebastian picked up the telephone and dialled the Rue de Fleurus, where he got Robert Bessy (who was just about to go out but, naturally, would be around at once). Smiling, he turned back to Eleanor.

'Parisians seem to live by adverbs. They're always "just" on the point of doing something but will "naturally" be delighted to come around, and he'll "certainly" set about "actively" finding me a job, you'll see.'

'I'm going to try and make myself presentable,' said Eleanor, 'plumber or no plumber. Robert may not be particularly susceptible to women, but I don't propose to meet him in my dressing-gown.'

All at once she felt in a good mood. Sebastian was again fancy-free, there was Mme Schiller to look after them, and the flat had acquired a certain lived-in charm.

'Don't worry,' she said on her way to the bathroom, 'you looked after the summer. Now I'm going to take over.'

With a smirk on his face that indicated it was about time, Sebastian made himself comfortable on the red divan and leafed through M. Schiller's copy of the *Parisien Libéré*. He, too, felt as happy as could be.

Robert Bessy was a man of medium height, rather stout, dressed in a style too young for him, and he clearly had a passionate admiration for Sebastian. He kissed Eleanor's hand, apologized for not having found them somewhere better to live – they expostulated at this – and accepted the dregs of his own bottle in a toothbrush glass. He was about forty years old; public relations man for a fashion house here, a theatre there, organizer of innumerable Parisian functions, he seemed to think it perfectly feasible, if a little alarming, to co-opt Sebastian as a partner. He tried to give him a general idea of what the job would entail.

'It's a profession in which you need above all to be sociable, quick-witted, tactful, charming – in other words, all your qualities, Sebastian.'

Eleanor had become scarlet in the face in an effort to stifle her laughter. Sebastian was irritated.

'My sister's an idiot. I no longer know many people in Paris, and sometimes I'm a bit tactless; but as for charm and quick-wittedness, my dear sister, allow me to say that I can give you a point or two.'

'Oh, quite, quite,' said Eleanor, her laughter exploding.

'At first,' continued Robert Bessy, a little disconcerted, 'you'll be rather shocked by certain things. It's a world where the priorities are not quite what you're accustomed to. But you'll get used to it. All you'll need is a little patience.'

'And quick wits,' Eleanor interjected.

'It's all fixed, then,' said Sebastian regally, as though he were doing his old schoolfriend a favour. 'I'll start next week. That'll give me time to replenish my wardrobe, which leaves a good deal to be desired.'

A tiny spark of panic appeared in Robert's eyes.

'You haven't asked me anything about money,' he said. 'It's very much a hand-to-mouth profession, you know.'

'I trust you, I trust you,' said Sebastian gaily. 'You've never been stingy that I know of.'

The spark of panic became a furnace.

'All the same, I think I should warn you . . .'

'I never discuss money in front of a woman,' said Sebastian curtly, whereupon Robert apologized, beating a retreat, and Eleanor understood the strange ascendancy that her deplorable brother had over him, and had kept for twenty years. A few cutting remarks, like that one, in the name of good taste. At school, Robert must constantly have made the comparison, just as he did today, between himself, the cocker spaniel eager to please, and Sebastian, the intelligent greyhound. For, just as the impressions of childhood or adolescence are registered and engraved on the memory far more deeply than those of middle-age, so there are certain influences, certain attractions, mental or physical, which, if experienced at the tender, that's to say the awkward age, continue to exert their power thirty years later. Perhaps because what really attracts us in these unhappy years of our youth is the unattainable, and Sebastian, to his friend, had remained and always would remain, despite the passage of time, Sebastian the unattainable.

Having found them a roof and undertaken to provide them with a means of livelihood, Robert Bessy could hardly do less than invite them to lunch, which he duly did. It was a very gay lunch. Eleanor was in her best form and attracted looks from all sides in the luxurious restaurant to which Robert took them. Noticing this and, in spite of his unqualified devotion, having a fair idea how this pair of cuckoos had been living over the past fifteen years, Robert thought with relief that he might not have to go on paying Sebastian very long for pretending to work. Already he was thinking up a few well-planned dinner parties which might relieve him of his responsibility. At the same time he thought nostalgically that ten years earlier he would have been overjoyed at the prospect of working with Sebastian, even of watching him go through the motions, because of the spice it would have added to his life. Yes, ten years ago, at thirty, he would still have been prepared to take all kinds of risks, and share them with someone he admired. In the meantime, though, he had been successful, had acquired responsibilities, and had managed to carve out a niche for himself in this cruel and exclusive Parisian world. As he chewed his lobster, he wondered sadly whether the expression wasn't only too horribly apt and whether this niche, so carefully hollowed out, wasn't also his tomb.

Chapter Eleven

A red February sun was setting behind black trees. From the window of her house in Normandy, the wretched scribbler watched the day drawing to its close. During the last forty-eight hours she had failed to write a single word. She ought to have been very unhappy about this. Trying to write without success was like making love without pleasure, drinking without getting drunk, travelling without ever arriving. It was being locked in limbo. True, the days went by imperceptibly, indistinguishably, and the weather, calm at last, was exquisitely mild, almost ecstatic in its stillness. All the same, she must live, work, return eventually to Paris, to 'other people'. She must pull herself together. Meanwhile, the sunlit mornings were beautiful, the earth was touched with frost, the dog played with a stick for hours on end, and the log fires crackled in accompaniment to the mammoth English novel, so rashly begun. Pull herself together . . . But she'd have to be unhappy first. It was only too true, though: the whole thing was becoming a painful chore. When she was eighteen, she had written a nice little French composition that had been published and had made her famous. She had refused to take it tragically, even seriously; in any case, writing was *a priori* a pleasure to her. And here she was, eighteen years later, obliged to take herself very seriously indeed if her situation, and that of her household, was not to become tragic. And yet she hadn't the slightest desire to write. Already, remorse for not having done 'a day's work' was weighing on her conscience. Taxes, debts, all sorts of lugubrious topics came between her and her poetic reveries. One lets things happen to one, easygoing habits develop, one lets other people compose an Identikit picture of oneself, one lets everything go, time, money, love-affairs, and one finds oneself in front of a typewriter as dumb as a worn-out accountant. And always, in counterpoint, that hint of inner laughter directed against oneself. That self-mockery. Oh yes, she readily admitted that she drove with bare feet – like everyone else, in fact, on the way back from the beach, because sand in your shoes is uncomfortable – oh yes, she readily admitted that whisky was one of her most faithful stand-bys – because life is not exactly kind to those half-flayed creatures known as human beings. Oh yes! But she wouldn't ever apologize for anything, as there didn't seem to her to be anyone worth apologizing to. At the most, in certain private and intimate circumstances, she might ask forgiveness in the dark, with true humility, of someone she had hurt. But to apologize for this amiable doll-like creature she was supposed to be, and perhaps in fact was, sometimes without realizing it, not on her life! One must cherish one's effigies, if one can tolerate them, perhaps more lovingly that one cherishes one's intrinsic self. That's the ABC of pride. And of humour.

'I, me, myself . . .' Whistling with happiness, the Good Lady of Honfleur glanced out of the other window: the cows still grazed the short winter grass, the dog was playing with his stick like a lunatic, the trees were spread out against the sky, and all was still. No birds, no ideas. As a matter of fact, she was more likely to be awakened the following morning by the song of birds than by the bubbling over of her ideas. She slept like a log here, her damaged arm stretched out beside her, at an angle, like another person. Waking in the morning to find it numb – since the poor thing really was fractured – she felt like comforting it, even shaking it by the hand. Her determined indifference to physical pain and her no less determined benevolence towards herself sometimes worried our scribbler. Schizophrenia, like a bat (*calva sorices*), was flying low that year. That would be the last straw. For, after all, just as she had had her wounds stitched up without an anaesthetic, with a sort of detachment that was totally unsimulated, so she couldn't settle down, for instance, to read, without making herself a little nest of pillows, cigarettes, Kleenex, a little nest that still never seemed to her quite perfect enough for her beloved self.

The Good Lady of Honfleur gave a deep sigh: a night bird, the first, the one that went 'hulihuli-a', had burst into song. The sun had vanished and she needed a drink. She had done no work. 'Another day wasted,' she said aloud, but something inside her, as she looked at the already darkened lawn, murmured: 'Another day saved.' Life sometimes offers such breathing spaces, when one can look at oneself in the mirror with a slight smile, half condescending, half conspiratorial, without demanding anything more than to be alive and at ease with oneself, while the evening bird goes 'hulihuli-a'. But these breathing spaces are rare: the tigers in our different engines are quick to come to life and tear one another apart.

Chapter Twelve

'The telephone hasn't rung for three minutes,' said Sebastian. 'It's delightful. Don't you think so, Mademoiselle?'

The secretary looked at him uncertainly. All Robert Bessy's colleagues put on a show of being busy, made telephone calls themselves if the instrument stopped ringing, and called her 'honey' or 'Elisa'. This tall, quiet, nonchalant man was as unlike a public relations man as it was possible to be. She even found his courtesy disconcerting: he helped her on with her coat, got up to light her cigarettes, and seemed quite unaware of the breezy style that prevailed in the firm. He had only been there three days and already the office had changed. People had stopped shouting and running and muttered 'sorry' whenever they bumped into one another in doorways. Whatever would M. Bessy say when he got back from New York? Moreover, the rare telephone calls that this M. van Milhem received were strange: some were from his sister, to whom he talked as though she were his mistress, and some from Mme Jedelman, his mistress, with whom he adopted the tone of an elder brother.

'Monsieur van Milhem,' she said timidly, 'you won't forget Bruno Raffet at six o'clock, will you?'

'Bruno Raffet?'

She sighed. Bruno Raffet was the star, the white hope of the Bessy stable. He was twenty-five, excessively handsome, and not untalented, and the film magazines talked of no one else. She got up and fetched the Raffet file and put it down in front of Sebastian.

'Perhaps you'd better read this,' she said. 'He's pretty well-known and rather touchy.'

Sebastian smiled, opened the file, and looked admiringly at the splendid animal that strutted through its pages.

'He must be attractive to women, wouldn't you say?' he inquired.

A deep sigh gave him his answer. He noted the regular features, the heavy lidded eyes, the dazzling teeth, the silky, wolfish air that was visible even in these glossy photographs. A greedy wolf, at that. Unfortunately, he had seen none of his films.

'What am I supposed to talk to him about?' he asked.

She shrugged her shoulders.

'I don't know. It's Monsieur Bessy who, er . . . discovered him, and he often comes in to ask for, er . . . advice.'

She was blushing slightly. Sebastian, remembering his friend Bessy's inclinations, thought that this wolf cub must lead him quite a dance.

'What advice do you think I ought to give him?' he asked gaily. 'Aside from continuing to brush those beautiful teeth twice a day . . .'

'I didn't know where to find him to put him off.'

'It should be fun,' said Sebastian.

And fun, in fact, is what it was. Because Eleanor, finding herself in the neighbourhood, stopped in to collect him and they waited together for the young film star to arrive; because Eleanor was in a very good mood and went out of her way to be nice to poor Elisa, who was fascinated by her; and because Sebastian's 'colleagues' came in, one after the other, to be introduced to her. Perched on Sebastian's desk, one of her long legs touching the ground, Eleanor accepted the homage of one and all. An atmosphere of well-bred refinement, of Versailles-like courtliness, began to reign in these gloss-painted offices where hitherto efficiency had been the byword and the only demonstration of respect a slap on

69

the back. In the midst of all this the young wolf arrived and paused on the threshold, astonished and rather nonplussed, sniffing the air before entering. Sebastian noticed him and decided that he was a natural-born actor whose looks were not entirely synthetic. Bruno Raffet was indeed very handsome: he had a mat complexion that flushed as easily as a boy's, very blond hair – one was tempted to say a very blond pelt – and big, rather heavy hands that, curiously enough, one could imagine becoming delicate and slender by the time he was forty, for professional reasons. He had in addition a little blue mark in the white of his left eye that gave him a predatory look at times, as though, having burst a blood vessel in his eye by dint of constant wariness and watchfulness, this go-getting young man had turned into a veritable beast of prey. He asked politely for Robert Bessy and, visibly intrigued, shook hands with Sebastian. He faltered only when confronted with Eleanor. This woman wasn't one of those starlets who were always cluttering up Bessy's office, nor what is nowadays referred to as a society woman (in other words, a rich woman whose wealth is acceptable), nor a script-writer. Who could this be? As for her brother, this tall vague ninny so out of place in these surroundings that he suddenly wondered if dear Robert hadn't fallen for him – he didn't help to clarify matters.

In the days when he had gone hungry and thirsty, as hungry and thirsty for glory as for a sandwich, Bruno Raffet had had what are known as pederastic relations with Robert Bessy. But his notion of pederasty was exclusively bound up with the idea of comfort. When he awoke in a man's bed, he could be sure of finding an electric razor, a bathrobe that fitted him, a particular mode of expression, vigorous or extravagant, that was always the same. In a woman's, on the other hand, he awoke to a breakfast tray on his knees, a lace napkin tucked under his chin, an admiring housemaid, and he would depart no less content but a good deal less well-shaven. Sex, then, for Bruno Raffet, had so far been confined to its 'Ideal Homes' aspect. Blessed, moreover, with a keen sexual appetite, and being himself easily satisfied, and having retained the ability to sleep like a child and wake up reasonably lively, he was the prototype of that breed, bisexual until the age of thirty, who can equally well beat someone up in a café for a perfectly justified remark or allow himself to be beaten for the pleasure of some elderly gentleman or pink-haired lady. Uncertain product of uncertain times, he had but one certitude: that the money he pocketed was indispensable, undeserved and, in any case, his for the taking. Consequently, when he came up against the wall of indifference that lay behind Eleanor's eyes, Eleanor's demeanour, he was no less taken aback than Christopher Columbus on first coming across the simple savages of North America. He was still young enough, or vulnerable enough, to be puzzled by it; and Sebastian, seeing this, knew that he would suffer. Nothing could be more disastrous for a young wolf than to come across M. Seguin's affectionate but inaccessible she-goat* – but a M. Seguin 1972 vintage of course. He knew in advance that even if he succeeded in biting Eleanor she wouldn't bleat in protest, and that the morsel of her flesh that he carried away would leave a special and no doubt irreplaceable taste in his mouth. All this was determined between them from the moment he was introduced to her, but only Sebastian was fully aware of it. He might have been no more than yet another young animal to Eleanor, but what she noticed first of all, and what committed her to this affair, was the minute blue mark and the white speck in his eye. Because of this she ascribed to him the affectionate and clumsy character of a dog she had had as a child. Eleanor much preferred dogs to wolves these days, not because of her age but as a result of various experiences. It was on the basis of this double misapprehension, animal-sentimental and

* *La Chèvre de M. Seguin*, from *Lettres de mon moulin* by Alphonse Daudet.

intellectual, that their love affair was launched. To complete the bestiary, Sebastian, perched behind his desk like an enormous owl, seemed implicitly to have appointed himself guardian of their nights and days.

How square I am – not one of my heroes takes drugs! But when you come to think of it, it's an absolute farce that in our day and age, when all the great taboos have been overcome, when sex – and its adjuncts – is a source of taxable income, when fraud, theft, and dishonesty have virtually become drawing-room jokes, people should be rapped over the knuckles for this one thing: drugs. They will tell you, of course, that alcohol or tobacco are as bad, if not worse. Personally, I'm on the side of the authorities for once, because if one is at all familiar with that world, one realizes that only one in a hundred thousand recovers from drug addiction, and at what a price, after what damage! The popular image we have of it clearly demonstrates this – and popular images, in their naïveté, are nearly always closer to the truth than abstract arguments. There is a world of difference between the cheerful drunkard in a bar, fat, reeling, and repulsive, true, but his face 'lit up' as they say – another popular image – and the gaunt young man alone in a room, his hands trembling as he plunges the syringe into a bulging vein, the difference being the absence of 'other people': the dipsomaniac gets pickled openly and the drug addict hides himself away. However that may be, it's not my intention either to eulogize alcohol or to attack drugs in the name of morality; I'm interested only in whether they make people happier or sadder. And besides, the nub of the matter lies not in this differentiation but in the cruel and undeniable fact that nowadays human beings, whether intelligent or stupid, sensitive or insensitive, lively or boring, are generally the victim of one of these dictators: alcohol, drugs, or the chemist (tranquillizers). As though life were nothing but a long, greasy road, down which one slides at terrifying speed towards a dark, unknown tunnel while desperately trying to establish footholds which one after another give way, whether their names are whisky, librium, or heroin (and realizing that the last-named needs renewing more often than the rest and is less reliable). Absence of religion, pollution, lack of ideals or lack of time, relations between men and women, false security, et cetera, et cetera – the litany of whys and wherefores that is chanted to us makes perfectly agreeable hearing and is almost reassuring in its monotony. But in the last analysis, why do you, I, me, myself, we, they – like some terrifying declension – whether we're twenty or fifty, whether we're rich or poor (and don't start telling me about the peasants: the sale of tranquillizers has multiplied tenfold over the past two years in the provinces, and in the most quiet rural districts at that), why do we always find ourselves, at any given moment, with our hand stretched out, not towards our fellow creatures, but towards a phial, a tube, or a bottle? It isn't the ever-increasing sum of human anguish that disturbs me: I imagine that it has always existed and that even the most beautiful, gifted, and erudite Greeks must occasionally, by the shores of the world's most beautiful sea, during the greatest period in the history of their beautiful country, have flung themselves down on the sand, torn their hair, and bitten their nails in terror. No, what disturbs me is that today all they would require is an understanding doctor, a prescription, and one of the six thousand or eighteen thousand bottles of tranquillizers, to calm them down within ten minutes. What disturbs me above all is the idea that they wouldn't even go and roll in the sand: they'd have some Equanil in their peplums.

Chapter Thirteen

Eleanor and the young man were dancing in a night-club . . .

Help! What have I said? Here I am back in Sagan-land and night-clubs! It's an odd experience for me these days as I read the newspapers to see the extent to which an author, whether he's called Troyat or Jardin or what you will, has only to introduce his characters into a night-club for the critics immediately to invoke my poor little name. As for the wretched author who has the temerity to extol the charms of a sports car, I wish him luck. The majority of the critics are appalling hypocrites. What could be more enjoyable than to drive in the sunshine in a beautiful open car, its engine growling at your feet like a caged tiger? What could be more enjoyable than to know that a whisky on the rocks awaits you at a villa on the other side of this golf course, among people as lively as yourself, and as free from material worries? What could be more natural, after all, than this search for and discovery of an agreeable spot, away from pressing problems? Yes, what hypocrites they are, these people! There's nothing disgraceful about money as long as one spends it, or throws it out of the window (preferably when there's someone passing underneath). In other words, as long as one turns it into something gaudy, baroque, absurd and, naturally, liquid. Money is only disgraceful because of the way it's earned and above all the way it's hoarded. I'd like to see those cheap demagogues saying the opposite to those who really know: people who travel second class would surely much prefer to arrive at the aforementioned villa with its ice cubes and its mimosa. Except that they're not invited, for reasons which may offend justice but which mean that they will never be able to accept our cheerful assurance that they are the righteous ones in the matter, and the blessed.

So, Eleanor was dancing in this night-club with this blond young man with the golden future, a future of fame, fatigue, old age, and oblivion – one of those glorious destinies in which one recognizes one's face in newspapers one despises – at least at the outset – and which one bitterly resents later on when one no longer appears in them. Actors are a bit like that and so, often, are writers, painters, film directors, anyone who has been in the limelight.

So, Eleanor was dancing with Bruno, and their movements swept them across the dance floor, the music flowing over them, carrying them along with it; and Bruno's evident desire combined with Eleanor's apparent indifference directed their steps into patterns and rhythms that they would never have discovered otherwise, together. She enjoyed retreating as he advanced, she liked the feel of his thighs hard against her own and his slightly dazed expression that meant one thing only: 'I want you.' Behind all this – all of which she was accustomed to – she sensed the terrifying phrase, 'I can't answer for anything.' She smiled when he suggested a drink downstairs, away from the noise, away from Sebastian, who was deep in conversation with God knows who. The cloakroom girl was a friend of Bruno's, and on the way downstairs he gave her a familiar sign before taking Eleanor into the telephone booth, one hand on her shoulder and the other around her waist. He had had rather too much to drink, and he no longer knew quite who she was or what he wanted from her, especially after that dinner with people whose elegance, wit, and gaiety had been too much for him, people for whom life and the pleasures of living had been reduced to a fine art. He wanted to give this woman a shock, to leave his mark on her. But when he drew her towards him, it was she who, laughing gently, kissed his moist neck and put her hands to his belt at the same moment as he did. Eleanor's eyes glistened in the dark for an instant before she closed her elongated lids, and then they let themselves drift, engulfed in a world of discarded clothes, warm hands, gentle caresses, the whole accomplished with a kind of deft skill that was astonishing because devoid of cynicism, something he had never experienced before. Some time later he came to with his head on her shoulder, his eyes closed, or rather clenched with pleasure, marvelling that her mouth could be so fresh. As for Eleanor, looking at this passionate young animal, she thought to herself that it was a long time since she had taken such a risk. (She was unaware of the connivance of the cloakroom girl, and she had always loathed scandal.) But the boy had had to be assuaged, and she knew that the only way to reassure someone lay in pleasure shared. People are so easy and relaxed after making love: a hand on an arm or a hip in the dark, the sleeping figure stretching, sighing, going back to sleep. No one should sleep alone. Live alone, perhaps, but not sleep alone. She knew that there was no danger in the raw experience of life, which could be hard, of course, and sometimes tedious – but at least kept one from dreaming, except where there is passion (and that in itself is a battle, often cruel but at least clear-cut, or at least governed by clear-cut rules). On the other hand, her tumultuous dreams and wild awakenings at dawn, her heart pounding, alarmed her much more. Those agonizing dawns described by Rimbaud, whom she had read thanks to Sebastian and whose work she knew better than that of any other poet. She wasn't afraid of dying, for to die is nothing in itself, no more than cutting a final wisdom tooth. It was the image of death that she was chary of. In her dreams and, what was worse, in the images she projected of them, Eleanor saw death as a relentless figure with a haughty profile, dressed in grey lace and a hat, and laughing politely at inanities like any well-mannered person at a dinner party that is dragging on and from which she will attempt to slip away civilly, but taking you with her in the process. Her absolute revulsion stemmed from this: she really thought of death as a monstrous old lady who comes to violate us, slowly in the case of illness, suddenly in the case of accident, but always bent on violation. For her there was no such thing as a heroic death. No one can die well or even at peace. One clings on to everything, one's agonies included, even people afflicted with 'a long and painful illness' as the papers say. (Strange, the press will openly use the words 'erection, bedpan, hepatitis, bladder', but never 'cancer'.) Such false prudishness is slightly nauseating. Oh yes, my mistake, one may talk about lung cancer: that's tobacco. Anyhow, for once it has to be acknowledged that Eleanor, the beauteous, aloof Eleanor, as unapproachable as the Princess of Aquitaine whose name she bore, had rediscovered in this young stranger, whose profession and whose photographs, whose likes and dislikes she had at first despised, something so violent, so desperate, so panic-stricken that she was profoundly touched by it. There are people like that, wounded without having received a single blow, and while they still hold all the cards – and here, I suppose, we must go back to Freud, to their little mummies who failed to give them enough affection, to their wicked daddies who slept with their little mummies, and to themselves, listening, wide-eyed in the dark, to the sounds from the conjugal bed, in short, to all the folklore, sometimes justified, more often boring, and in any case humiliating. If, by the age of fifteen, I hadn't recognized the fact that my parents' love for one another was also physical, I would have been not only a fool, but *a posteriori* an ungrateful one.

I'm beginning to mix everything up, Eleanor and myself, her life and mine, and this is only natural, such being my intention, as the faithful reader will discover should he reach the end of this weird lucubration. So I shall leave Eleanor, her knees trembling a little in the telephone booth, her arms around the neck of a young man she scarcely knows but whose impulsiveness appeals to her. Now that she knows his weight, his smell, his breath, she won't hesitate to go to bed with him. Eleanor has never had any time for progressive women – or what are known as progressive women. As far as she's concerned, men are clumsy, attractive, inconsistent, silly, or touching. She doesn't give a damn for Women's Lib. Equal work, equal pay, yes. Naturally enough, since in any case she doesn't work. The whole thing bores her. And then men sleep so nicely; they sleep like dogs (gun dogs) or like hedgehogs, half curled up, or like superb lions, sprawling and snoring; but always, if you're fond of them, with a non-chalant, proprietorial elbow in your stomach so that you can't sleep. And we poor women, our eyes open in the dark, we support this weight, so close, so dictatorial, without stirring a muscle. Ah, there, yes, when there's a leg lying on top of yours for hours and giving you pins and needles, there you feel, long live Women's Lib! Until a lonely hand, a naked hand as Aragon would say, stretches out towards you, childishly or tenderly, and grips yours. The ways of love are all the same, whether infantile, childish, sexual, tender, sadistic, erotic, or whispered. It's simply a question of understanding, of understanding oneself above all: in bed, in broad daylight, madly or not at all, in shadow, in sunlight, in despair or at table. Otherwise, it's no use. Any of it. And the little time we have left for living, while we're still alive, in other words capable of giving pleasure, and the little time we have left for thinking (or pretending to) in this vast, mindless cacophony that daily life has become, ineluctable, uncontrollable, and truly unacceptable to any civilized person, we must make absolutely certain that we share. There are even times when I long for, yes, long for the advent of that steel-grey aeroplane, the sudden roar of the engine, a little too loud, the stunned faces raised towards the sound, and the black package, hardly visible, that will drop from it. I've come to long for the explosion, the shattering of the heavens, of our eyes, our eardrums, and even the unimaginable furnace and the primitive, inevitable cry, grotesque in our age of technological progress: 'Mother!' The only thing I'd be afraid of, should this horror befall us, would be finding myself alone in an empty house. To die, yes, but to die with my nose buried in someone's neck while the earth explodes or is ruined beyond repair. I believe I'd have a feeling of pride, of wild delight, of poetry – the last, unique opportunity to realize that within me there was a backbone, a defiance, a passion for others or for love or what you will, and that God was powerless against it.

I'm raving, I'm raving and talking nonsense, but so what! I'm feeling rather carried away, after two days in Paris in the company of sensible, practical people whose lives are so well organized that they're dying at top speed, and even, horror of horrors, aware of what's happening to them. No fun in life for them. All the poets were nocturnal creatures, alcoholic and unhinged. Truly, we should buy shares in Shell and washing machines in order to be respected and sure of living to a ripe old age. And comfortable in the withered bosom of our old age? No, thanks! Long live night-clubs, and long live the merry or melancholy solitude of those who huddle together therein! Long live the false and true warmth of a false and true friendship struck up there! Long live the false tenderness of chance encounters and long live, finally, what everyone else does in slow motion but which we, the night-prowlers, do at a gallop, speeded up: the discovery of a new face, a wild affair, a romantic friendship, the brotherhood of alcohol on the brain replacing the brotherhood of blood on the wrist! We're not noble savages any longer. What of it? We're tired Europeans. And that is why, to get back to the point at last, Eleanor was momentarily dazzled, on the evening in question, by the excitement, and the desire to conceal his excitement, exhibited by that unpromising child who was now, at twenty-eight years of age, the number one hope of the French cinema, Bruno Raffet.

Chapter Fourteen

March 1972

Out of the window of my train, between Deauville and
Paris, I can see a placid goat sitting, literally sitting, all
alone, beside a glinting stream. Further on, three men
stripped to the waist, two of them alabaster white and the
third bronzed and handsome, are burning the stubble (and
their fire, eclipsed by the pale sun, only burns brighter – a
haemophiliac fire, as it were). Tut, tut, what a pretty piece of
prose! I used to want my life to be one long, classical French
essay: quotations from Proust throughout, from Chateau-
briand in the holidays, Rimbaud at eighteen, Sartre at
twenty-five, Scott Fitzgerald at thirty. I've left out a few, of
course, too many indeed, and too deliberately. My life in fact
is like a hurried, slap-dash essay of the kind written by the
hopeless pupil who has never learned to quote, except from
time to time, for her own pleasure, her own satisfaction, and
her private enjoyment. Indeed, I live at such a rate that now
I can no longer distinguish the months or the years, and the
deliberate movements and the cigarette butts of those itin-
erant farm workers seem to me to represent the height of
luxury. I too, on the whole, am living slowly at the moment.
But I have the impression that they remember every instant,
whereas for me these six months spent working in the
country have become a waltzlike blur with glimpses of trees,
first black, then dark green, then apple green, and of birds, at
first shy and shivering under grey skies, then chattering and
preening themselves against a sky reddened by the early
spring sun. In case I am thought unduly sensitive to the

seasons (cf. this book: 'Ah, what an autumn, ah, what a spring'), it's only because there was no winter that year, 1971, over that frozen ice rink of time, between the two seasons.

Lying on her stomach in the unfamiliar bed, safe in the knowledge that her back was shapely, golden, and smooth to the touch, Eleanor examined one after another the weird objects that were strewn about the floor of the room. There were carved wooden heads, more or less African in origin (mostly less), there were a few pieces of pottery, there was what she detected as being a sense of taste – or more precisely a notion of taste – on the part of this tasteless young man. He had instinct, but not an iota of taste. He was one of those men who make a beeline for the people they need, or who need them, or who simply attract them, but who, faced with a work of art, stand there waving their arms, demanding dates, details, references that they would never dream of asking from any human being because they would already know (from instinct) his entire life history. Eleanor, who had been slightly put off by Bruno Raffet's rumoured reputation for a certain degree of homosexual aestheticism – since nothing depressed her more in a very young man than collector's mania – found this total lack of discernment in what were clearly very expensive purchases a distinct recommendation in her new lover. She could tell that the bogus eccentricity of this flat, far from being dictated by the taste of some elderly protector, reflected the lack of taste of its owner, who had scattered everything indiscriminately for the admiration, whether malicious or merely ignorant, of all comers. It made her laugh, but her laugh was gentle, compassionate, and almost tender. He was sleeping at her side, his head hunched between his shoulders, as tense in sleep as he was during the day, and for a moment she pitied him from the bottom of her heart for being inevitably doomed to

be a flesh-eater. One day, unless he fell victim to the pan-
oply, the curtain-fire of alcoholism, drugs, and the rest, he
would be one of those men-dogs trained to jump at the
muzzles of Leicas and television cameras, one of those men-
dogs who, like their female counterparts, will roll over on to
their backs, waving their paws in the air, at the mere suggestion of a front-page photograph. Meanwhile, he was good to
look at in the morning light, surrounded by his fetishes acquired from some ritzy junk shop, all the better-looking,
indeed, for the fact that these old wood carvings were fake
whereas his young skin was genuine, all the better-looking
for the fact that the intellectual effort, so absurd and pretentious, that he had made to acquire some genuine carvings
had failed. Within ten years he would either be an impover-
ished has-been or, quite possibly, a cultivated man. And all
he could rely on, in order to pass from one stage to the next,
if all went well (this latter stage being regarded as privileged), were his most gratuitous qualities – his skin, his dazzling eyes, his sexual potency – and his basest – his ambition,
his lack of scruple, and his mercenariness. Eleanor, who, as
we know, cared nothing for such things, since culture, elegance, and above all disinterestedness had been hers from
the cradle, also knew that these attributes were the pre-
rogative of a particular human breed – not noble in the her-
aldic sense of the term – but people of whatever social
background who, to put it crudely, are always ready to
empty their pockets; and she was seized with a curious tenderness for this over-endowed young stranger. Not for a
second did it cross her mind that he might one day make her
suffer. He had too many trump cards, she no longer had
enough; he valued those he held too greatly, she no longer
valued those she had left. In matters of love, it is worth
remembering that the only indestructible *Panzer*, the only
long-range gun, the only unavoidable mine and, horror of
horrors, the only nuclear bomb we cannot hurl at the other

person, the bomb that *ipso facto* horribly prolongs the battle, is indifference. She had behind her a stockpile of such weapons sufficient to lay waste the rich pastures of this young man's torso and those flanks of his sown with golden hairs like harvest corn; she had enough rusty artillery to aim straight at this heart beating in the dark next to her own. As for the bomb that she hoped she would never have to use, it was the simple little phrase, so overworked these days, her private sentimental Hiroshima, 'You bore me.' And the vanquished victor, in his deep childlike slumber, with his blond hair and his fists clenched before his face in an instinctive gesture of defence, perhaps against her, perhaps against a former life of which she knew nothing, filled her with a sort of gentle melancholy on her own account. It was time she went back to Sebastian, the ideal brother who was distant yet always within reach, ineffectual yet equal to anything, crazy and yet so wise, aloof and yet so considerate, insecure and yet so confident, this living paradox, the only man, not whom she had ever loved but who had ever intrigued her. She left the sleeper surrounded by his mute African heads, some of them terrifying in their ancient malevolence on the brand-new carpet, she left the handsome young man asleep, knowing that he might wake up at any moment; and, like a Cocteau heroine, she telephoned for a taxi in an urgent whisper, the sort of voice one uses to summon a priest or some undesirable ex-lover. Then, leaving her romantic stage whisper in the telephone receiver, she ran down the stairs whistling an old tune from Offenbach that had suddenly come into her head not because it fitted her mood but because it fitted the rhythm of her footsteps on the staircase. Like Sebastian two months earlier, she walked a little way in the blue, dazzling, Parisian dawn, reflecting, as he had reflected, that she had emerged unscathed, but forgetting that the very fact of her posing this question to herself meant that it was no longer true.

Chapter Fifteen

That same morning, a morning that had none of the wanness of dawn since the autumn was unusually resplendent, it was Sebastian's turn to wait. He had watched Eleanor allowing herself to be captured by, or more exactly capturing, the young man. He had laughed about it at first, then had begun to wonder; and finally, he had been hurt to the quick at being left on his own in the flat, like an orphan. Such a thing had never happened to him. Over the past six months, without realizing it, he had grown accustomed to being the one who went out; and to be the one who stayed at home, or rather waited up, was extremely painful to him, and somehow anomalous. To take his mind off it, he picked up a pencil and began listing all the different forms of absence that he could think of. (When things were going badly, or not too well, Sebastian had the healthy impulse to analyse the reasons and write them down.) His neat summary went as follows:

1. The absence of x when one doesn't love x, but x remains absent nonetheless (cf. Proust). Here, the imagination can begin to wander with unforeseeable consequences ranging from sudden passion to total indifference.
2. The absence of x when one loves x and knows one is loved in return, but x remains absent. Now here, the imagination runs wild: 'Is he dead, in prison, lying hurt somewhere?' This is the authentic lover's nightmare.
3. The absence of x when one knows one loves x but one

isn't sure of x's feelings. This time one is not so much terrified as horrified: 'Where is he? Has he done it on purpose? Is he having a game with me? If so, what and why?'

Sebastian found this catalogue both relevant and soothing, and he lay down, fully dressed, on the nearest bed, because for some obscure reason he didn't want to be undressed when his sister returned. Perhaps he was always playing a part. He tried to ignore the howl of loneliness that welled up inside him as he thought what his daily life, in essence, amounted to: Nora Jedelman, whom he now visited only out of pity, a job in which he couldn't decently believe, and now the physical absence of his alter ego, Eleanor. Not that he disapproved of or even for a moment pictured to himself the pleasures from which Eleanor was just then extricating herself – he knew only too well that pleasure exists only in loving, at any rate the pleasure he regarded as valid, and he knew equally well that for the moment it was out of the question that she could be in love with this youngster – but he would have liked her to be there, he would have liked to be sharing a nightcap with her, to be having a chat with her, to be holding a post mortem on the evening, in short, not to be alone any more. The howl, or rather the throb of loneliness was no longer merely nagging: it was obsessive. Until it seemed that God himself should have blocked His ears, except that God's ears would have been blocked long ago if He had any. Between the cries of children and the cries of adults from bombing and from hunger, in this century or another, that miserable and sadistic old man would have had a severe cramp in his arms. I hate the idea of God, any God – I hope believers will forgive me – but then, why do they believe? Is He really necessary? Or at any rate, why did He have to make Himself necessary solely by way of compensation? And yet I swear I was once a Catholic, collecting holy pictures and even singing, in a convent in 1943, among other things, 'Nearer, my God, to Thee' in the same breath as 'We're with you, Marshal Pétain.' Come to think of it, between the ages of four and six I was an exemplary child, healthy in mind and body, pious, guzzling my turnips along with the rest and chanting my prayers as enthusiastically as all the other children of my age. (Later on, it's true, I became less healthy and less pure, thanks to life and the dearth of turnips.) But then there was this ghastly vision, in a country cinema to which I was taken by mistake when still very young, that caused a new person to be born within me. I won't dwell on it – Dachau, with its bulldozers and its corpses, and everything that nowadays compels me to leave the room whenever I hear the slightest anti-Semitic remark and makes me incapable of tolerating a certain kind of talk and even a certain kind of cynicism – and God knows I've developed a deliberate cynicism of my own over the years, with the life I've led and the people I've known. It's a *sine qua non* for me – and I'm ashamed to say so in an age where everyone wears their fine sentiments on their sleeves as ostentatiously as their ignoble ones – that I would cheerfully (cheerfully is an exaggeration, but at any rate deliberately) face a firing squad rather than say or do certain things, or allow them to be done. It's also a *sine qua non* that I don't esteem myself one jot the more for this, having never cultivated in relation to myself anything other than the perpetual and diabolical desire to please. Never the desire to be respected. Respect leaves me cold, which is indeed just as well, since what with my driving Ferraris in bare feet, my drinking, and my dissolute life, it would be most extraordinary for anyone to consider me worthy of respect – unless at some time or other they have been struck by a phrase in one of my books and want to tell me so. But even then it always seems to me that this phrase, this affective missile has been fired at random and I can no more claim responsibility for it than for the air we breathe. I don't think it's all that important to preserve one's self-esteem or to think of oneself as an entity with precise distinguishing marks. I merely think that one shouldn't put oneself in a contemptible position (by contemptible, I mean very precisely a position in which one despises oneself). I'm not talking about other people, needless to say. In this instance, the opinion of other people is as vain and ineffectual as the foam that slides harmlessly off the rocks. That isn't what wears you down. What wears you down is the wave, and the wave is the reflection of yourself glimpsed a thousand times in a mirror, and that reflection is a thousand times truer, a thousand times harsher than the reflection, too often indulgent, that lurks in the eyes of those famous 'other people'. Of course there have been times when I've hated myself altruistically, so to speak, usually because I've done someone harm. Of course there have been times when I've despised myself because I've failed to be any use to someone or to myself. Of course there have been times when I've been left stranded, like a fish out of water, gasping for air and for happiness, or for what the English call 'self-satisfaction'. What of it? The truth was never anything else but myself alone, hating myself sometimes for being alive at dawn, just as it was equally myself peacefully aware of my life, of the air I breathe, of my own hand lying apart on the sheet, at dawn on the following day. But, in either case, alone.

Depression may be rather too fashionable a subject, but it's nevertheless fascinating. I began this novel-essay with a description of that state. Since when I've encountered fifteen similar cases and I myself only pulled through by virtue of this curious habit of stringing words together one after another, words that suddenly began once again to blossom forth in front of my eyes and echo in my head. And each time I came across this malady, this catastrophe – for it's no joking matter, and nothing to do with laziness or weakness of will – I was overwhelmed with sympathy. As a matter of fact, when you think of it, why write at all if not to explain to 'other people' that they can escape this disease, or at any rate recover from it? The absurd, the naïve justification for any piece of writing, whether a novel or an essay or even a thesis, is always this outstretched hand, this frantic desire to try to prove that there's something to prove. It's this comic habit of wanting to demonstrate that forces exist, currents of strength, currents of weakness, but that in so far as any of this can be formulated it's therefore relatively harmless. As for the poets, my favourites, those who play games with their deaths, their feeling for words, and their sanity, perhaps they take more risks than we novelists do. It takes quite a nerve to write: 'The earth is blue as an orange,' and it requires colossal effrontery to write: 'The dawns are desolating/every moon is anguish and every sun is gall.' Because that is to play about with the only thing that belongs to us pen-pushers – words and their meaning – and it's tantamount to abandoning your weapons before the battle begins or deciding to hold them upside down and wait with your eyes already dazzled, half blinded, for them to explode in your face. This is what I have against the New Novelists. They play with blank cartridges, defused grenades, leaving their readers to create for themselves characters left undelineated between neutral words, while they, the authors, openly wash their hands of them. God knows, ellipsis is tempting. I don't understand the pleasure some writers get from using it to the extent that they do, but it's really a little too facile, possibly even unhealthy, to make people puzzle over obscurities when there's nothing to show that they've caused the author himself any real headache. Give me a Balzac, who weeps over his heroines, his tears falling into his coffee, or give me a Proust, who in his obsession with detail leaves no room for development.

After this little lecture on French literature, I shall return to my Swedes or, more precisely, to my Swedish lady who with her long legs is striding along the pavements of Paris in the early morning. I still don't know why I flung Eleanor into the arms of that young whelp. (No doubt because I find it difficult to visualize the outcome of this escapade.) Perhaps it was because I like spinning out my stories or because, consumed with a jealousy foreign to my nature, I'm beginning to be slightly irritated by her integrity and her way of defending herself in a love affair, resorting to a technique as implacable and effective as Modesty Blaise's judo. One doesn't admire one's heroes or one's heroines, one doesn't even envy them, since that would be pure masochism and masochism isn't my strong point. Or my weak one. Nevertheless, Eleanor makes me feel small. It's really true: I want her to bite the dust, to toss and turn in bed, sweating and biting her knuckles, to wait for hours by the telephone in case this Bruno boy should deign to call her, but I genuinely don't know how to bring her to this. In so far as she does whatever she likes, her sensuality is kept under control, and her loneliness is neutralized by the presence of her brother. And she has no ambition whatsoever. I shall end up on the side of Bruno Raffet, who, being what he is, remains vulnerable. As a matter of fact, I've often found myself preferring second-rate people to supposedly superior people, simply and solely because of their uncontrollable tendency to bang themselves against the sides of life's vast lampshade like fireflies or moths. And my frantic attempts to catch them in flight without hurting them, without crushing their wings, have never been particularly successful, any more than my ludicrous efforts to switch off the lamp in time. And then, some time later, whether it's an hour in the case of insects, or a year in the case of human beings, I find them still clinging to the inside of the lampshade, as eager to stun themselves, to suffer, to bash themselves about as when I had tried to stop their pathetic merry-go-round. I may appear resigned to it all, but I'm not; it's the others, the newspapers and television, who are. 'Oyez, oyez, good people. So many per cent of you are about to die in car crashes, so many per cent of cancer of the throat, so many per cent of alcoholism, so many per cent of a poverty-stricken old age. And don't say you haven't been warned.' Except that, in my opinion, the proverb is untrue and prevention is not cure. I believe the reverse: 'Oyez, oyez, good people, listen to me, so many per cent of you will experience a great love, so many per cent of you will understand something about your lives, so many per cent of you will be in a position to help someone, so many per cent of you will die (of course, a hundred per cent will die), but for so many per cent of you there will be someone in tears watching at your bedside.' That is the essence of this godforsaken existence. Not the beaches that unreel in the film sets of our dreams, not the Club Méditerranée, not playmates, but something fragile, precious, that we systematically plunder in this day and age and that Christians call 'the soul'. (Atheists too, in fact, without using the same term.) And if we're not careful, the day will come when we'll be faced with this soul, panting, begging for mercy, and covered with bruises ... bruises that we shall have richly deserved.

Chapter Sixteen

Like most of us, Eleanor had been born in the dark with the sheets of her mother's bed pulled up over her head and, like all of us, bunch of fledgling owls that we are, she had tried to put off uncovering herself for as long as possible. Since she wasn't poor, no one had snatched the sheets away from her brutally at too tender an age, and she had had plenty of time to edge her way slowly towards the light, or life. The only thing was that she had never emerged into broad daylight. Long before her looks and her innate qualities would have led anyone to expect, she had begun to pull the sheets back over her head and retreat into the security of darkness. In fact, but for Sebastian, she would have had no contact with life other than those, at once inhibited and unbridled, which she had with another naked body, and which must be as remote as possible from the raw, harsh realities of existence, whether poverty, passion, or violence. She was a dreamer without imagination, and this explained her weakness for books and her harshness towards her lovers. Cats liked her more than dogs. They recognized in her a sort of fatalism, an impersonal warmth, a life at once intense and inert that they had in common with her. Bruno Raffet, who was quite a different sort of animal, wolflike, eternally ravenous, unsatisfied and, on occasion, savage, was too immature to perceive this. To round off yet another metaphor from the animal world, if there had been a fire somewhere and their characters were reduced to their most elementary state, Eleanor would have approached it purring, while Bruno would have fled with his teeth bared. Meanwhile, they were driving along together in an open car, elegant and handsome as a pair of dummies, on their way to lunch at a rustic inn on the outskirts of Paris; and Bruno, unused to women of this sort, had adopted a manner that exasperated Eleanor in the extreme. He had thrown his keys to the gas station attendant, amiably it's true, but nevertheless 'thrown', he had given each tyre a knowledgeable, friendly kick, he had tapped the various dials on the dashboard of his little English sports car with a proprietorial air, he had even gone so far as to suggest to Eleanor that she light her own cigarette with the cigarlighter. She found it inconceivable that a man shouldn't stop on the expressway to light her cigarette. She found it inconceivable that someone should throw his car keys to a garage attendant, or to anyone else for that matter, instead of calmly handing them over; she found the whole sporting-driver's act that in his euphoria he was putting on for her quite ridiculous; indeed, she almost wondered why he hadn't cried, 'Gee-up!' as he let out the clutch. To complete the picture, disregarding the buffeting wind that was ruining Eleanor's make-up, he had taken it into his head to find some seductive tunes on his car radio which, he might have guessed, would be inaudible once he exceeded 70 miles an hour. The tiresome thing about a certain type of vulgarity (even if, in Bruno Raffet's case, it was mere childishness) is that it can suddenly be triggered off by a possession whose charm must at all costs be shared with someone who doesn't care two hoots for it. Bruno's ignorance about his African masks and his obvious indifference to them had endeared him to Eleanor, but he loved his car and, in her eyes, loved it in the wrong way. She had had many horses as a girl. It had never occurred to her to pat their heads or give them lumps of sugar. She had simply been concerned with treating their mouths well and schooling them. It was the best way she knew to pay tribute to their beauty, their strength, and their indifference. Now, years later, she wasn't going to go into raptures over a dashboard. Consequently, it was in a very bad mood that she took her seat at table in this pretentious inn, surrounded by what seemed to her ghastly people who talked either too loud or too soft and created, or sought to create, an atmosphere of exclusiveness or mystery out of these perfectly anodyne surroundings. Bruno was positively purring; he was delighted with the way things were going and privately thought himself rather admirable for having invited out to lunch, the day after he had 'had' her, a woman who could be of no use to him; he was feeling very much the young lord of the establishment and of the highway and of his prey. He handed her the menu with a lordly gesture, putting on the patronizing, not to say slightly bored, air of a man who knows that women, because they are thinking as much of their figures as their appetites, take a long time to make up their minds. This attitude was not only for Eleanor's benefit but for the benefit of the restaurant staff, who had immediately recognized the famous Bruno Raffet, and he examined his fingernails with an unassuming and indulgent smile. He was therefore surprised to see Eleanor's grey, unblinking eyes coolly taking it all in and even more surprised when she handed him back the menu as though she were giving a baby its pacifier, got up from the table, and vanished. He just had time to push his chair back, his manager having told him it was the thing to do, and sit down again – imagining in his proprietorial glow that she had gone to tidy her hair. *Perhaps she was feeling a bit faint, perhaps he had driven too fast, but what was one to do with no fewer than 300 horsepower under the bonnet and a clear expressway for once? Anyway, Swedish women were supposed to have strong stomachs.* After ten minutes or so, he began to get restless and found himself in what was, for him, a novel situation. Only recently, and not without difficulty (via God only knew what beds and what pitfalls!), he had made the transition from peevish, graceless, avaricious youth to blasé young man. This too rapid adjustment, so to speak, meant that he lost his head, nearly shook the headwaiter by the shoulders, interrogated the cloakroom girl over-anxiously, ran to his car, and then ran back again to telephone Paris, much to the amusement of the barman, who was already in on the story. This was the moment, while he was still totally unaware of her motives for deserting him, for him to make up his mind to forget her. According to the sort of clockwork mentality he had picked up from his managers, from newspaper articles, and from his various conquests, where a woman or a contract was concerned there shouldn't be the slightest chink in one's armour. But Eleanor had left in a taxi, and this put him back three years, to the time when he had gone hungry and thirsty, to the time when life was not, as it was now, simply what he wanted it to be. So, like the heroes in the storybooks, heroes he had always considered rather silly, he got into his car and sped back to Paris in hot pursuit. It was Sebastian, in a sweater, who opened the door. 'Yes,' said Sebastian, 'she's here; yes, she found the wind too much; yes, you know how it is, she isn't too keen on rustic inns; yes, you know what it is, sometimes she finds it difficult to explain; yes, she's asleep.' Then he had the impulse that was to save him; almost pushing aside Sebastian, who put on an air of indulgent scepticism, he opened the door and found Eleanor stretched out on the bed placidly reading *Pickwick Papers*. As he looked at her, certain memories and anecdotes of friends came back to him and he told himself that here and now he must show her who was the boss. Give a woman a good hiding and she won't do it twice. Alternatively, ignore the whole thing and pretend you don't give a damn; but it was too late for that since he had followed her back and was standing there trembling with fear and anger at the foot of her bed, in this dingy little flat that suddenly seemed to him the most forbidding and best-defended of castles.

'I see you couldn't stand that dreadful place either,' said Eleanor. 'Listen, I've got to the bit where Pickwick and his friends are on a battlefield during a manoeuvre. I've never read anything so funny.'

And as he stood staring at her, still windswept and stupefied with anger and amazement, she gaily patted the pillow beside her and, pointing to a passage in the book with her finger, virtually forced him to lie down beside her. He had never read *Pickwick*, and once his heart had stopped pounding and he could take in the sentences which she was reading to him in a low voice, punctuated with peals of laughter, he ended up by laughing too, snuggling against her, all tension gone, and so spent one of the best afternoons of his life. Around five o'clock, since they were getting hungry, Sebastian, who seemed to have abandoned his role of manager for the day, cooked them some spaghetti.

Chapter Seventeen

It may seem strange to begin a chapter with a marginal note, but something has been puzzling me since yesterday evening, when I first noticed it: why is it that in every detective story, as soon as a man on the run turns down the good offices of a prostitute in the street, we read, 'He repulsed her'? And, every time, the wretched woman hurls insults at him. Are prostitutes really so vain and resentful? Or do men take pleasure in the idea that, because they have refused their bodies or their money to women whose profession it is to solicit them (and often a very wearisome profession, I imagine), the latter must feel outraged and aggrieved? I don't know. In any case, as I say, it's an intriguing though minor point. On second thought, is it so minor? I believe men like to be desired by anyone, no matter who and for no matter what reason, even if it means dipping their hands into their pockets. Women, too, come to that. But it's more understandable in women: they're still, regardless of anything we may do or say, 'the object'; and an object is dispassionate, practically invulnerable, and all the more invulnerable because it doesn't attack. But those great babies, our masters, our Samsons, whom the world wants to deprive of Delilahs – for, after all, it's obvious that quite apart from their strength, we're going to be the ones who cut their hair at the same time as their hearts – in my opinion, they're getting a bad press these days. If I understand it correctly:

(*a*) They're the breadwinners – but that's unfair because they earn more than women.

(*b*) They take their wives, three children, and a dog for a drive at weekends, and they're endangering their wives in doing so.

(*c*) They make love, true enough, but on the one hand it appears that it's overrated (see *Marie-Claire* on the relative unimportance of their sex in the matter).

(*d*) On the other hand, should there be a slip-up, who's going to suffer for it? Not them! And that's grossly unfair to us, even if we've forgotten to take that precious pill with our morning coffee.

(*e*) They're unfaithful to their wives, they drink, and finally, they often prefer one another's company, which it appears is a sign of utter contempt for us.

(*f*) Having bought a television set, they have an unfortunate tendency to flop down in front of it, and in spite of the fact that we more or less forced them to buy it, this is a sign of boredom.

And, after all, we don't ask much of them: not to overdo the male role in life, but nevertheless to be a real man, and at the same time notice when we're wearing a new dress, go into raptures over it, and want us all the more as a result. As for the idea that we should reassure them about themselves, they shouldn't count too much on that. They've had two thousand years, even if they were only born thirty years ago, in which to oppress us, to prevent us from achieving great things, and it's about time they paid for it. I'm joking, of course, but much as I detest the ostentatious virility of some men who, it must be admitted, bore most women (by night as well as by day), there are times, especially these days, when I begin to feel some sympathy with their gentle and puzzled protests. How tedious this mania for generalization can be! It isn't the man we live with who's going to decide about equal pay, any more than it's he who'll decide the number of children we're going to want, any more than it's he who's the symbol of this famous sex war that we're always hearing about. It's too easy to enumerate absurdities on that subject – and God knows there are plenty, on both sides – but it seems to me regrettable, or more precisely, stupid, that for the sake of certain abstract theories, two people whose lives together have been based on concrete reality should be reduced to totally irrelevant and sterile debate.

But what am I saying? Either a man and a woman are intellectually compatible and can discuss why they like an article in a newspaper, or a poem, or a piece of music, or a particular horse in the Tiercé (and God knows it's rare for this desire to talk to one another to last beyond a few years!) or else their relationship is a purely physical one. 'Where are you? What have you been doing? I don't love you any more. I love you. I'm leaving. I'm staying.' What will these theories lead to? Splitting the human race into two on the pretext of reconciling it or unifying it or putting it on the same level, when one knows that men and women have always attained or fallen short of or transcended this level, depending on their relative strength or weakness, and that it's ultimately absurd. I've seen brutes loved by sensitive women, ferocious women by tenderhearted men, and so on. I've never believed that the notion of sexual equality could be valid, except, of course, as regards wages, and the kinds of quasi-racial discrimination which exist and will, I fear, continue to exist for a long time to come. If one acknowledges that all human relationships are based on a fundamental inequality – an inequality that cuts across sexual boundaries and that for me has been summed up in the most accurate and terrifying way by Huxley: 'In love, there is always one who loves and one who submits to being loved' – and if one accepts this cruel but inescapable truth, one cannot help but realize that inequality between the sexes isn't the real problem. And that's where a lot of intelligent and sincere women are taken in. The truth is that the married couple, or the individual, or the mass of people are completely deadened by a way of life that is designed to deaden them and that even if it weren't *designed* to do so would nevertheless succeed. And it follows from this, of course, in accordance with the prevailing technique – which is a technique of diverting the argument – that the inequality of the sexes is blamed for the mutual exhaustion of a married couple. For after all, which of us, man or woman, can come home after a full day's work and expect to feel anything but hungry, thirsty, and tired? (Except, possibly, during the first year of living together.) There was the same effort to misrepresent the profound and, to me, justified rejection by a generation of not unintelligent young people of a future that no forty-year-old, if he were honest, would accept. Oh yes, we hear them complain loudly enough today, our forty-year-olds: 'It's a disgrace, you can't call them beaches any more! There's no countryside left! There's no longer any freedom!' And if they were offered their youth over again, do you really believe they'd choose their children's? They'd find it intolerable. They'd insist on a playback of the long tape recorder of life and they'd begin again at exactly the same point as before. And it isn't lack of curiosity or a hankering after the past that motivates them, but a profound horror of a future which, if present indications are anything to go by, will certainly be no fun. And thereupon – the same technique of evasion – they explain that this generation loves violence, that it hasn't any constructive ideas, that it isn't even interested in love. And yet I've seen very young people deeply in love, in an ultra-romantic way, but no one gives them credit for it: 'No, no, if you don't mind my saying so, *my* generation knew all about feelings, we read Balzac and all the classics; and if my son cries himself to sleep, it's only because some little bitch who's been sleeping with all his friends anyway has cheated on him.' As for eroticism: 'These poor kids don't know the meaning of the word, whereas we, when we were twenty-five – d'you remember, Arthur? – we knew how to enjoy ourselves all right.' It's time you got it into your thick heads, dear bourgeois, whatever your age or whatever your class (for when it comes to love, the French, on the grounds of their glorious past, are ten times more chauvinistic than any other nation), it's time you realized that love between twenty-year-olds is not merely the contact between two naked bodies. What you must fundamentally recognize is that these young creatures, with the same inner urges, also want the warmth and the poetry – these desires being perhaps more quickly assuaged between the sheets than in the days of their elders, but quite as imperative.

In any case, thank God, neither this government nor its successors will determine how these young people will turn out. Their roots are already spreading, and those roots are derision, contempt, and not, alas, hope – not yet. It's easy enough to tell them, 'You wait, by the time you're our age, you'll be earning this much as an assistant manager and you'll pay that much for a family car; you'll see how quickly you'll be forced to change your tune – if not by us, then by circumstances or money, or rather the lack of it.' But in my opinion it would be more natural, and more affectionate, on the part of their elders to say, 'Go on, have a good time, but don't beat up your teachers or your pals – because really violence is an irreversible phenomenon and primarily a bourgeois one, and by practising it you'll wind up in the same mess as ourselves. Go and take a look at new places, go to the other ends of the earth, since that's what you're dying to do; forget all the folklore, go and visit the Hindus, hashish or no hashish, it's perfectly feasible; go and visit the English, too, and if you feel so inclined, treat the world as your playground since it's now yours for the price of a few dollars and a little time.' It's not easy to say such things to kids who are high-strung, complicated and, in many cases, already bogged down. But if they're bogged down, we must remind ourselves that we left them to their own devices, and that, during the nightmare of the past twenty years, there's been nothing to drag them out of themselves. Any more than for us. But we've had our chance to bewail our fate, and God knows we took advantage of it. Now it's up to us to help. Amen.

Disaster! I'm horrified to discover that I've completely forgotten a character en route: the poor man who was so fascinated by the back of Eleanor's neck in the Rue Pierre Charron and who was destined to play a strange and obsessive role in her life. Now he's been overlooked and, having done my best to get interested in him again, I can see that he won't last the distance. Ah well, too bad. Whatever my original Machiavellian intentions, he'll have been a man who, in a sunny restaurant, once stared at Eleanor's profile. His role stops there. Anyone can mislay the odd protagonist along the way, but out of politeness and before expunging him forever from my pages, I'll give this one a name: he's called Jean-Pierre Bouldot, a bank clerk for the past twenty years, extremely badly paid and, as the saying goes, a good citizen. He pays his taxes on the dot, not without a struggle, his wife is frigid, his children rather below average, and he takes the Metro every day from Aubervilliers. At one time, being an engineer *manqué*, he anticipated that the improvements on this line would be interesting from a technical point of view. He hoped that human intercourse would be simplified as a result and that it would be a joy to him to go down those steps every morning and climb them again every evening. Unfortunately, it was all a bit too complicated and technical, and his loudly voiced enthusiasm found no echo among his fellow passengers. Nevertheless, he's making out all right these days: he lives with his Metro ticket between his teeth and he gets home in the evenings in time to pacify or smack his children as the case may be. On the day he saw Eleanor, he had been squeezed in so many turnstiles, had taken so many wrong turnings, had sweated so much and got so out of breath in that labyrinth, which had become transmogrified into the most terrifying wilderness in the most savage western, that he had got out, defeated, at the Champs-Élysées. And there, a beneficiary of progress, no doubt, but unable to think up a better excuse for his boss, M. Colet-Roillard, than an attack of 'flu' (an excuse that would in any case debar him from the office for the afternoon), he decided to lunch in a snack bar in the Rue Pierre Charron. It was there that he had seen Eleanor as one sees somebody one has always known and yet will never know. Long afterwards, having endlessly daydreamed between the Metro stations that bounded his habitual journey and the inexorable path of his destiny, he had succeeded, at the time of writing, in forgetting Eleanor completely. Exit Jean-Pierre Bouldot.

Chapter Eighteen

Bruno, meanwhile, was blissfully happy. He had infiltrated the van Milhem camp. He was at once teased and supported by Sebastian, who was rather amused by him, and accepted by Eleanor, who no doubt confined herself to giving him her body. But when he awoke at her side and tried to awaken her too with little affectionate, interrogative nudges with his head, he marvelled to see her look of surprise, to see her yawn and turn to him, flat stomach against flat stomach, hands on one another's backs, and he marvelled, too, at the quickening of her breath – something that only his caresses could provoke. For none of his words or his thoughts seemed to annoy, to touch, or to humiliate Eleanor. Pressed against her, his blood coursing through his veins, he waited peacefully, unsuspectingly, for her to give him the push. It was then that Robert Bessy returned from New York. He had had a trying three weeks, business had been tough, and he had had to swallow large quantities of tranquillizers in order to keep going. He returned to Paris in no better shape than when he had left: viz., short, fat, and unsure of himself. His only solace was the thought of his friends the van Milhems, the beautiful van Milhems who had never in their lives felt the lure of the dollar, and of Bruno, rather too good-looking, rather too unstable, whom he had raised to his present not inconsiderable heights by dint of patience and generosity. His feelings for him were perfectly disinterested, inasmuch as he never expected any physical response from him and inasmuch as he, Robert Bessy, at the age of forty, had become as vulnerable and helpless as an infant. There was no one to meet him at the airport but there was a message in his flat, the flat in the Rue de Fleurus in which Eleanor and Sebastian had lived, the flat he had kept on because it was the scene of his first meetings with Bruno, a flat that was now empty, lifeless, without even any flowers, a thousand times more depressing in its Englishness than the van Milhems' present stark abode. There is a kind of comfort, of luxury and well-being which is perhaps only bearable when there are two or more people to share it, and which when you are alone, like Robert, becomes positively hostile. What was the use of those two Regency chairs in front of an empty grate, what was the use of that splendid view over the rooftops, what was the use of that impeccable, all-electric kitchenette, of the valet on which he hung his overcoat, of the suitcases with their exotic lables, TWA, NEW YORK, PARIS, and above all, what was the use of his unshaven face reflected in the mirror? He tried to pass off his depression as the effect of the famous jet lag which is a familiar excuse among travelling people. Petty astronauts, they have been quick to confuse the deficiencies in their blood stream with the great clichés of the day: time, distance, nervous exhaustion. He took some pills, half stimulant, half sedative, and went through the motions of bathing, shaving, and changing his clothes, like a sleepwalker. He had arrived at three o'clock in the afternoon, local time, but he felt as though it was midnight, the witching hour. Instead of telephoning his office, he sat down on his bed, incapable even of unpacking, and waited. An hour later, an hour in which it seemed to him that he had plumbed the depths of misery and loneliness, the telephone rang. It was Sebastian, Eleanor, and Bruno calling from a bar: they hadn't wanted to disturb him earlier, so that he could get a bit of rest. (Good intentions have much to answer for.) He made an effort to sound cheerful and bright, but when Bruno said (his voice seemed different, somehow),

'If you like, "we'll" come and pick you up . . . if you like, "we'll" meet somewhere . . . if you like "we'll" come to you,' he knew there and then, without a shadow of doubt, that the faint blows to the heart he received with each 'we', and the absence of a single 'they', were merely the prelude to a great, painful tattoo that would leave him no peace. They were 'other people', and therefore hell. He was himself alone, washed, dressed, and shaved, awaiting his summons, in other words his sentence, an hour and a half later. What was more, he told himself bitterly, it was really nobody's fault, not Bruno's because he knew perfectly well that Bruno preferred women, not Sebastian's, because *he* had never been able to take such matters seriously, not Eleanor's, who had never hesitated to take anyone she wanted, and who, had he mentioned it to her, would certainly have handed Bruno back to him at once. But no one can ever give anyone back to you: *finders keepers*, that's the rule. Something that he, Robert Bessy, nice, kind Robert Bessy, had never been able to manage. In going out to meet this formidable trio, he felt like Daniel on his way to the lions' den. Except that Daniel was handsome and slim and young and soon had the lions at his feet. These lions of his would buffet him gaily and kindly with their elegant pads, bristling with claws that were never sufficiently clipped and filed. Without knowing what they were doing, they would cut him to shreds and send him back alone to this flat where there was no living thing left to look at except his suitcase. As a precaution, he put two extra pills into his waistcoat pocket and then sat down to wait; looking down at his feet, at the black tips of his beautifully made shoes, bought for thirty dollars at Saks Fifth Avenue, splendid moccasins off which he had, as it happened, brought back an identical pair for Bruno, he waited for nightfall and the sacrificial hour.

The town is empty and I wonder, half fascinated, if the

people will ever come back. I know they're all on the roads, in their different machines, driving towards pleasure or possibly death, while I feel comparatively free and safe. I compare myself to the bird which lives just opposite me, my nearest neighbour in fact, and which has pitched its tent in a tree that has been sawed to the bone, a tree that nevertheless looks horribly alive, more so, even, than the rest – those burgeoning with leaves, buds, and promises. This particular tree, being totally bare, looks mutilated yet is nothing of the kind. At any rate, for this reason or for reasons of comfort which the cuckoo understands but I don't, this tree is thronged with birds. In the spring, to my intense displeasure, more aural, I admit, than sentimental, they came with a buzz saw – I think that's the term – to amputate my neighbour. For trees are always pruned at dawn, in Paris. Daring workmen, perched at heights that made me tremble as much from fear for their safety as from rage at my loss of sleep, cut these poor chestnut trees to pieces.

As though to reassure it – I'm still speaking of my tree – the birds chose the forks between its sawn-off members as so many sanctuaries. It is much more popular than the other, living trees. Which reminds me, I wonder where I shall take refuge later on. There are so many different ways of dying and so few of them are elegant. To be sure, there's always 'the ceremony of crumpled steel', as Blondin wrote of Nimier;* there's an old-fashioned, peaceful old age by the fireside somewhere in the country with obstreperous grandchildren climbing over your knees; there's suicide, that slippery slope that mustn't be talked about; there are also farcical solutions. If I've always refused to be a member of any kind of jury or to take on what are called responsibilities in the literary world, it's not so much out of principle as out of a laziness which has become a principle in itself. Today, however,

* Writer Roger Nimier died in a car crash and his obituary was written by his friend Antoine Blondin.

perched on my balcony and watching a snarling dog, an exasperated father, and a tearful child go by, I can well see myself in years to come, an amiable old lady covered in decorations of every kind, and still a bit confused in my diction (there's little hope that things improve with age), sitting in state at a banquet at Drouant's, or at Maxim's, I'm not fussy. I'm seventy-four years old. My fourth husband has just died, stupidly as they say, so I'm dressed in black and my decorations show up all the better. I've just finished a little sole with lemon juice, because my doctor forbids all excess. Some television commentator or other interviews me, not without difficulty as my glass of Chablis has gone to my head. Nevertheless, I tell him how praiseworthy the latest prize-winning novel is and how delighted we are, my colleagues Duras, Mallet-Joris, and myself, to have honoured a new talent. At which point I begin to squawk, because I haven't had my raspberry flan and I've grown very greedy with age. Benoît IV, my latest chauffeur, impassively helps me on with my Pomeranian stork coat (the latest fashion-fur in 2010). The prize winner, decked out in moa-feathers, covers my hands with kisses. Benoît IV opens the door of our aerocar and, after passing other aerocars belonging to friends on the way, we alight on the terrace in the Rue Guynemer. For some time now, the Invalides–Champs-Élysées hop has come to resemble Zola's Champs-Élysées without the horse droppings. Lecanuet is still in power, thanks to the remarkably efficacious injections by Dr Jekyll. On the Côte d'Azur, because of pollution, vacationers are not allowed within five miles of the shore. Ah, the things I've seen, the things I shall see before I die! I've seen women turned savages burning their bosses' files on the Place de la Concorde. I've seen children threatening their parents with the whip, refusing to allow them the slightest sexual deviation. 'Beware of traumas!' they cried, and the happy, docile parents, relieved of responsibility at long last, trailed behind these little self-intoxicated gnomes whose principal object it was to deprive them of all sustenance. I've seen 'the hourglass of earth and sky turn upside down' (cf. Éluard). I've seen exotic plants growing happily in Paris. I've seen people madly in love accept the fact that their love is unilateral. I've seen people give the shirts off their backs to their friends, knowing that the latter would never know. I've seen farmers reading poetry as they lolled beside their grazing cows, and shouting to me as I passed, 'You know, the earth is blue as an orange!' I've seen fish drunk with despair (usually gudgeon, I don't know why) fling themselves, eyes upturned, on to the hook. I've seen owls hide and refuse to open their eyes for nights on end, so fed up were they with our bliss.

Chapter Nineteen

'How about some caviar?' asked Robert.

He was one of the last survivors of an underfed generation for whom the words 'caviar' or 'champagne' still had festive connotations. Eleanor, unfortunately, had never liked caviar. Sebastian found it didn't agree with him. As for Bruno, now that he knew he could have it whenever he wanted, he no longer had more than a condescending flicker of interest. The three of them surrounded him, as in a dream, affectionate but very remote, and he tried to ingratiate himself with each of them in turn, like an unpopular little boy in a school playground. Bruno first, of course. Superb, dazzling Bruno, blonder and more blue-eyed than ever, like one of those characters in Proust, of whom he had only read the biography; as though his new passion for Eleanor had, by some strange alchemy, intensified his natural colouring, making it more resplendent. For there could no longer be any doubt that he was now very much in love with Eleanor. All his gestures were directed towards her, and the restrained graciousness with which she received his compliments was even more disquieting to Robert. Her attitude clearly revealed that she was not yet in love with Bruno, that she lagged behind him, in other words had the edge on him. And as Robert knew only too well, having always fallen in love too soon, this small time lag was generally irrecoverable. Sebastian was doing his best to understand poor Robert's troubles, but he had a natural tendency to take things light-heartedly; and in any case there were a thousand possible explanations for the panic-stricken expression that occasionally came over his friend's face: the journey, exhaustion, irritation, possibly even the affair between Bruno and Eleanor, an affair to which he personally attached little importance but which might turn out to be more serious than he thought. After all, Robert must have known that Bruno preferred women, that Eleanor wasn't his first mistress, nor his last, and that the nonchalance with which his sister treated her love affairs was a guarantee of safety for the future. As for Eleanor, she was doing her utmost (out of consideration for Robert) to channel, even to stifle, the exuberance of her young lover, and her aloofness was more accentuated than ever. This naturally made Bruno even more passionate than usual, and more impatient. He could think of no explanation for this coolness which he found so hurtful, and it never occurred to him that Eleanor might know of his former relationship with Robert. Young people, however cynical, have these prudish inhibitions and assume that everyone else shares them. By the same token, not having the remotest idea why he was being made to suffer in this way, he now decided that it was Robert's fault, he being the extraneous element introduced into their charmed circle after a fortnight's absence. All of them were right in their way and all of them behaved well. But alas, there was this crucified animal on the pink tablecloth, in this restaurant, and that animal was Robert. The caviar having been turned down, they were offered *caneton aux olives* and then cheese, also turned down, followed by a *sorbet*, which was unanimously accepted. Each of the courses, and especially the intervals in between, was an additional torture for Robert Bessy. At one point he fumbled for his tranquillizers (the ones he had had the foresight to slip into his waistcoat pocket) and swallowed them with a hearty laugh, explaining that American food, however healthy, gave him heartburn. They decided on a final drink in a night club, and the word 'final' made Robert jump as though it were an obscenity. Nevertheless, he caught himself picking up the bill for his expense account, conscientious businessman that he was, and it made him smile. What an incredible farce it all was! His whole life had been just that. His natural good will, his ebullience, his infatuations and, a little later on, his inclinations had combined to make a horrible jumble of the remainder of his life, each moment of which could only wound him further. He sat there in the taxi with his eyes open, perfectly clear-headed for once, no longer looking at, no longer even seeing, Bruno's hand clasped over Eleanor's in the shadows. The club they had chosen because it was 'fun' was like Dante's Inferno or something out of Hieronymus Bosch. But he said 'hello, hello' nevertheless, he shook hands all around, and when an old crony pointed to Bruno with a wink, he smiled gaily with a knowing air, just as he had done three years before. The music, the smoke, the alcohol were no longer pleasantly vertiginous excitements but cruel and unavoidable compulsions which would never again be capable of breaking his fall. An hour went by that seemed an eternity, Sebastian dozing, Eleanor dancing as little as possible and finding even that too much because Bruno plagued her with questions as soon as they were alone. Robert waited. He waited for the *coup de grâce* that couldn't be long in coming. When they left, the van Milhems, deafened and rather jaded, announced that they would walk home together, by themselves, and having embraced him warmly, vanished into the night. Bruno, without looking him in the face, hurriedly explained that he had a long-standing date with some friends and that he would ring him next day. Left alone, Robert called a taxi, and as it drove off he saw, without experiencing the slightest additional pain, that Bruno had walked around the block and was running like a madman towards Eleanor's flat, that little flat that he, Robert, had unearthed one day the previous August thanks to his concierge, not knowing that this somewhat seedy abode would become his lost paradise.

Whether from exhaustion due to the effects of those apparently fatal time zones, or from some deeper compulsion that he could suddenly no longer ignore, Robert Bessy killed himself that night. He swallowed, without difficulty, the rest of his pills, and by sheer chance the dose happened to be sufficient to do the trick. As they say in detective stories, he knocked himself off. A rather vivid piece of slang in the sense that, having knocked up against life, he had been unable to rise above it. Often, on a racetrack, superb thoroughbreds knock into a fence, are unable to get up again or damage themselves in doing so, and the vet has to come and put them out of their misery. Robert Bessy was neither superb nor thoroughbred, and he dispensed with a vet.

Chapter Twenty

I have placed my heroes, then, in the most hellish, the most unbearable, and the most odious position: that of feeling responsible for a death one has in no way desired and in no way foreseen. When, earlier in this book, I wrote an apologia for imagination, it was of course for this reason: happiness and unhappiness, recklessness and gaiety are all perfectly wholesome states of mind, perfectly valid and necessary, but they make one blind. The situation of my two Swedes and my young Frenchman, learning, at dawn, of the death of their friend from despair and desertion, is one from which there is positively no escape. Sebastian was sad and accused himself of being more imperceptive than he really was, of being brutal even, for in such situations one prefers to invent faults for oneself than to acknowledge one's failing. Eleanor felt out of place. As for Bruno, the most closely involved, having the cruelty and honesty of youth, he thought of one thing and one thing only: the consequences that Robert's death would have upon his relations with the van Milhems. I shall have more to say about that later on, but meanwhile it would be as well for people who commit suicide and don't allow you to ignore it to realize once and for all that it isn't sorrow, real sorrow, that they generally leave in their wake; nor is it remorse. And yet that is always their aim. What they produce is a defensive reaction or at any rate a desperate attempt at self-justification. This means that those most closely affected, whatever their genuine distress, are much more concerned with explaining to others how they hadn't realized, how they couldn't have realized ('You know what she was like'), in other words more concerned with forging an alibi for themselves than mourning the dead. God knows I've seen plenty of suicides in my life. Admirable ones, tidy ones, sordid ones, unsuccessful ones, second attempts. It's a subject on which I no longer know what to believe. It isn't true that people never try again after an 'unsuccessful attempt'. It isn't true, in my opinion, contrary to that of the psychiatrists, that there are born suicides. On the other hand, I certainly think that once a person has made up his mind to draw attention to himself in this particular way, all other ways are closed to him. Given that the aim of ninety-nine per cent of human beings (and I'm being generous) is to draw attention to themselves, one could almost draw up statistics, and in the more extreme and frenetic cases define quite precisely, by means of some mock national opinion poll, how many had chosen sleeping pills, how many seduction, how many pride. But there's a real nightmare for those left behind, and that is the 'if'. The conditional, the conditional tense as it is conjugated, has always irritated me in the extreme. As far as I'm concerned, the phrases 'if only I'd known' or 'if only I'd understood', etc., have always been meaningless, conjecture without the benefit of experience, and thus patently inadmissible. 'If pigs might fly . . .' has always seemed to me the height of idiocy, mockery, and contemptibleness, because after all, if we knew why we were alive, if we knew why someone we love dies, or, which is perhaps even sillier, if we knew why someone we love no longer loves us, then we'd really be getting somewhere! The real horror of a friend's suicide is that the 'if' one propounds yet once more is suddenly fixed, or at any rate locatable in space and time: 'It's ridiculous, when I left Arthur at three o'clock, he seemed perfectly all right. If I'd known that . . .' 'It's absurd, I passed him just opposite the Flore, he was brown as a berry, and he waved at me. If . . .'

And the multitude of tiny memories that everyone digs up for your benefit begins to seem like a bunch of sharks determined to have the hide off you, and the bones. All these memories are pinpointed, and are therefore unbearable. For instance, supposing I read in the newspaper that Arthur has been killed in a car accident (since it appears to be the most fashionable way to die); well, depending on my relations with Arthur, either I bang my head against the wall, or I telephone his mother, or I weep, or I simply say, 'Poor old Arthur, he always was a bad driver.' But if the same Arthur has finally decided that life isn't worth living – and my life too, in a certain sense, since he's a friend – and if no one has been able to prevent him from putting an end to it, neither his friends nor my friends nor even me, and Arthur is lying dead and cold somewhere, I end up by wondering sometimes whether Arthur, my Arthur or yours, didn't have the right idea. When you kill yourself, you not only shatter people's hearts, their affection for you, their sense of responsibility towards you, you also undermine their basic reason for living, which, if they really think about it, is no more than an intake of breath, the flutter of a pulse, and now and then a moment's ecstasy at the contemplation of a garden, a person, or a plan, however ridiculous. It undermines everything. Suicides are very brave and very blameworthy. I have loved too many of them to pass any definitive judgement, and in any case, who am I to judge anyone? But certain decencies, such as a simulated accident, in private of course, still seem to me more humane, nicer – the word is inadequate and that's what I like about it – than this business of flinging your corpse in people's faces as much as to say: 'There you are, you couldn't do a thing to stop me.' If only my neurotic friends would leave me in peace nowadays, if only they'd put some Schumann or some Wagner into the mini-cassettes in their *deux-chevaux* or their Ferraris, if only, in the name of heaven, they'd pretend! Decorum, let's have a little decorum! Just because life is inelegant doesn't mean we have to behave likewise. Why can't they spare us the pills, the pistol shots, and above all that disfiguring gas; why can't they spare us all that and do us the kindness of allowing us to believe that life for them was a thing of charm and beauty and exotic delight, that it's only by an unhappy chance that it has been wrested from them, and that now, six feet underground, overgrown with weeds, they envy us for still being there to enjoy it. That seems to me to be the least one can do for the people one loves, the people one has let down. However, I can't lay down the law on this subject because like everyone else, circus dogs that we all are, I've jumped through the burning, golden hoops of that temptation, like everyone else I've felt fear and longing, and like everyone else I would gladly, at times, have made further attempts at those hoops and trampolines. Since then, something has happened to change me, either a faint distaste for the whole business or a faint renewal of my taste for myself or, quite simply, fear. The imbroglios that people contemplating suicide involve themselves in are both the most high-minded and the most obscene conceivable. If I've chosen to speak rather boldly about this poor man's death, it's because I have a horror of this sort of self-pitying scream, a scream which in his case would doubtless have been 'Bruno', 'Mother', or 'My God', or 'I'm in pain', or 'I'm thirsty', a scream which means that death is never triumphant.

The rain was coming down in buckets, and in a gloomy church in the 16e *arrondissement*, endeavouring to follow a ritual unfamiliar to them as Protestants, stood the van Milhems, upright, blond, and pale with exhaustion, not knowing when to raise or lower their heads and caring even less. A few rows away was Bruno, who hadn't seen them again till then. For the rest, there was that delightful cohort which, on various pretexts, is to be seen at every christening, wedding, or funeral in Paris and would, if it could, attend divorces as well. Press photographers went up and down the aisle taking what they call discreet flash photographs. And the priest, who had clearly got the message that suicide was no longer an impediment to a Christian burial, said Mass in French. In his sermon he explained to all the long-faced people in the congregation, in a theatrical idiom one would no longer dare attribute to any lady professor at the Comédie-Française, that they would never again see their friend Robert Bessy on this earth, that he would disappear into the clouds but that, thanks be to God, there would be someone somewhere to take him in, comfort him, and ensure his eternal happiness. To anyone who knew that for Robert Bessy, this eager, fond comforter had been and could only be that frivolous young nitwit Bruno, the idea was calculated to provoke a smile or floods of tears. The Parisian approach to funerals is both solemn and grotesque. People arrange to meet beforehand, lunch together, and hold each other's hands. After which they whisper a few lugubrious comments on the absurdity of the priest's sermon, and then comes the extraordinary moment, undoubtedly the only genuine moment, when they see the person who believed himself or herself to be the Robin Hood or Joan of Arc or God knows what of their generation, pass by in a cramped little wooden box. They are well aware that this little box awaits them too, and that one day, as a result of smoking or driving or suddenly succumbing to one of life's innumerable hazards, they will find themselves therein, horizontal in the midst of vertical people who will have been whispering more or less continuously throughout the Mass. As the coffin goes by, it's the one moment when you see people's faces crumple, whether because they've lost someone they've loved and are now remembering, or because they're afraid for themselves. The van Milhems were afraid of nothing, and in any case they had lost something that was, for them, irrecoverable: this corpse was nothing less than the corpse of their luck, the corpse of their good nature, the corpse of their insouciance, and worst of all, of their nobility of soul. They had inadvertently allowed one of their friends to kill himself, and although they had never mentioned it between themselves, even at the time the blow happened – and it was a real blow – for anyone who knew them well their demeanour betrayed a hundred unspoken comments, each more terrible than the last. Robert Bessy, like so many typical Parisians after they had died, turned out to have a father and a mother in the provinces who were as nondescript as every other provincial father and mother, and who bore themselves with dignity. Everyone, impresarios, producers, film directors, actors, friends, went up to pay their respects to this somehow exotic couple who had no idea that their son was homosexual, solitary, and snobbish and that that was why he had killed himself. And Robert Bessy's mother thought that the most friendly, the 'nicest-looking' person in the congregation was Bruno Raffet. Afterwards, everyone went out on to the forecourt. The coffin was swiftly embarked – since undertakers in France have this in common with the Sanitation Department: they work at top speed – and then, in the driving rain, some people went off to find their cars – because after all, a car is always useful even when one is grief-stricken (especially when one is grief-stricken) – while others looked for taxis. Bruno, his hair soaked to the scalp and looking handsomer than ever, came up to the van Milhems, who were standing there, aloof, remote, and abstracted, like two exotic birds, and for a moment he hoped their lack of involvement in that appalling Mass, their apparent indifference, meant that he still had a chance. But as he lifted his woebegone face to Eleanor's, as though somehow imploring her help – in an almost childlike way, as though to say, 'You know I've done nothing wrong; anyhow you can't blame me for loving you, for having loved you' – at that moment gently, almost tenderly, Sebastian pushed him away with one hand, like a commissionaire, and wagged a finger at him that was not at all a sign of complicity, but, on the contrary, a sign that meant that he really must give up there and then. Eleanor didn't even look at him. She had an old muff dug up from God knows where, and an ancient toque drenched by the rain, and altogether the van Milhems, apart from the proud carriage of their heads, it goes without saying, were less elegant than usual. Bruno was never to see them again. He knew perfectly well that it wasn't his fault, and that they didn't regard it as his fault or theirs either; it was simply that the van Milhems had failed somebody who was their friend, who had looked after them like a friend, and to forgive themselves for this was out of the question. In any case *she* couldn't forgive herself for it in the arms of his executioner. Even if he had only become an executioner because of her.

Chapter Twenty-one

April 1972

I met them that same night. They were getting deliberately drunk and so was I. They looked fairly battered and I was too. I didn't know their problems, but I had enough of my own. I began to tell them about a house in Normandy that was windswept, ringed by trees, full of dogs and cats – I should say one dog and one cat, since one shouldn't have dogs and cats in the plural: that amounts to a denial of animal jealousy, a denial I deplore. Anyway I was telling them about this house. I told them that the wind made the shutters bang like mad, that sometimes it was fine during the day, that the sea was nearby, and that all things considered it was, or could be, an ideal refuge. We left the date fairly open and so I was very surprised when, the day before my departure, they telephoned, still wanting to come. In the meantime, I had heard their story, or at least the story of Robert Bessy. I'd heard of Bruno Raffet's incessant and fruitless telephone calls, I'd heard what people said about them, about what was called their 'arrogance', and I liked what I heard. So we set off in a hired Mercedes, with luggage that was almost as frayed-looking as its owners, and took the road to Normandy. Nothing much was said during the journey. For reasons I didn't know and never had time to discover, the chauffeur was the most talkative, the gayest among us. It was as though we were all trying to find some elementary form of politeness and niceness. Each of us, it seemed, needed bandaging all over.

They liked the house. It's a big house and the wind does

indeed howl around it. And it isn't very elegant, so everyone can put their feet on the sofas. The first night was odd. We recognized one another, of course. But each of our words and gestures might have been interchangeable, so much so that we spoke to one another with extreme politeness and almost avoided one another. Drink had become a balm, music a 'background' as they say. As for the dog, clumsy and affectionate, gazing steadily at us and evidently puzzled by these three humans who should have been dictatorial but were merely speechless with fatigue, he seemed the only living creature among the lot of us. My own scar being the least serious, during the course of this evening overclouded with politeness and reciprocal wariness, I made up my mind to try to help them. 'Tomorrow,' I told myself, 'everything I can give them shall be theirs. I shall give them the grass, my precious grass, I shall give them the goat with no ears, who's bound to make Eleanor laugh. I shall give them a sort of peace, a sort of rebellion, anger, and indignation, I shall give them everything I've been able to do or to achieve over thirty-seven years; I shall try to give them, if I can, some way of coming to terms with themselves at the same time as I myself try to do the same.' But tomorrow was tomorrow and I think that the night seemed long to each of us in our separate rooms.

From then on it rained without ceasing. Sebastian and I, too weak to resist, got into the habit of sleeping together with or without good reason. At all events we spent our days at Eleanor's feet, while she remained as ever engrossed in her detective stories, looking oh, so elegant compared with us, so dirty, so dishevelled, so human. From time to time she would run her beautiful long fingers through our hair, comparing the texture, the softness, and thus we became, he, her brother, and I, the stranger, rivals in laughter and more affectionate than ever. We listened to nothing but opera: *La*

Bohème, Tosca, La Traviata, and the sublime voices of the singers allied to the simplicity of their emotional problems pierced our hearts. The trees along the drive dripped with rain, to such an extent that the dog preferred to play indoors with us rather than out of doors with his sticks. The fire crackled, inviting from one and all confidences that we never brought ourselves to exchange. It could have been a life, perhaps – a strange life but nonetheless genuine because utterly free of compulsion, and when Eleanor's slender hand brushed my cheek and Sebastian's head rested on my shoulder as he hummed '*Mi chiamano Mimi*', yes, it added up to something. Something quiet, tender, and doomed from the start. There should be reserves for the pure of heart, as for Red Indians. My country house was close to being that, because I watched over it as scrupulously as my over-affectionate dog and my over-watchful cat.

Then came Stockholm. A telegram from Stockholm. I remember that afternoon. I was sitting, as usual, on the floor, between Eleanor's and Sebastian's knees, all of us helpless with laughter, and I heard the postman arrive. The telegram said that Hugo had been released at last and that he, the only man who had never, even for one minute, doubted Eleanor or her love, was waiting at Stockholm airport for her to come back to him. She got up and I understood her. I understood at once her desire to go back to this man who was wrong about her, her desire to go back to this interminable misunderstanding and this reassuring madness. For I could tell from her eyes, from her gestures, that she was at the end of her tether, that she had had enough of the shoddy Paris of 1972 that her brother had tried to enliven for her. With the telegram, she breathed again, they both breathed again. Back to the peaceful rivers of Sweden, back to Hugo, so generous in his foolishness, back to worlds I had never known. Nevertheless, the last evening was painful. We were all three of us in the little sitting room, the cat in Eleanor's lap, the dog stretched out on the floor still breathing God knows what scents of the chase, but breathing heavily between Sebastian and me. Then, overcome by tiredness and tension, we said, 'Goodnight, see you in the morning,' knowing that the morning would bring one of those farewells made hectic by the pressure of time and urgency, for the train left at a quarter past twelve and we were not the sort of people who are wide awake by a quarter past twelve. It was indeed a painful journey – from my house to Deauville station. When I say painful I mean silent. We had five minutes to spare and we spent them with our noses buried in one another's necks. I didn't know who was who any longer, nor did they. And then that stupid train began to puff and smoke and make trainlike noises. And suddenly, peering over that thing like a bannister rail, I saw those two faces once more, very distant and yet at the same time so tender that I knew I would never see their like again. I raised my hand. It was pouring rain but neither of them begged me to go, and I said in a rather faint voice, 'Au revoir, au revoir.' Eleanor van Milhem leaned forward (and the Normandy countryside shimmered around her in the window pane) and she said to me, 'No, not au revoir, good-bye,' in a voice so gentle and so final that I could have taken it the wrong way if I hadn't known better. The spring had been very cold in Deauville that year. Nevertheless, as I left the station, alone and feeling rather sick at the thought, it cleared up, thanks to one of those happy storms peculiar to Normandy skies and, on my way to my car, I received a pitiless shaft of sunlight on my face and I knew that Eleanor was right, that it was the last time I should see the van Milhems face to face, and perhaps myself as well.

More About Penguins
and Pelicans

Penguinews, which appears every month, contains
details of all the new books issued by Penguins
as they are published. From time to time it is
supplemented by *Penguins in Print*, which is our
complete list of almost 5,000 titles.

A specimen copy of *Penguinews* will be sent to you
free on request. Please write to Dept E P, Penguin
Books Ltd, Harmondsworth, Middlesex, for your
copy.

In the U.S.A.: For a complete list of books available
from Penguins in the United States write to Dept
C S, Penguin Books, 625 Madison Avenue, New
York, New York 10022.

In Canada: For a complete list of books available
from Penguins in Canada write to Penguin Books
Canada Ltd, 2801 John Street, Markham,
Ontario L3R 1B4.

Françoise Sagan

La Chamade

Four people. A woman who has not known the
passionate turmoil of love for ten years; and
suddenly encounters the need for just such a love.
A man with devotion enough to let her go. A
younger man with desire enough to keep her too
close. A woman who watches, tautly aware that
impossible indifference must hide the hurt within
her.

Four people, jaggedly emerging from the superficial
gloss of the Paris social set, each drawn out by
Mademoiselle Sagan's impressive insight into real
life and real love. La Chamade? The roll on a drum
to announce defeat. But whose is the victory?

Also published:

Aimez-vous Brahms . . .

Françoise Sagan

Bonjour Tristesse

A book that comes straight from the heart of a girl
involved in a dangerous game to wreck her father's
plan to re-marry.

'This is not just a remarkable book for a girl to
have written; it is a remarkable book absolutely . . .
She is marvellously gifted' – *Sunday Times*

'A work of art of much beauty and psychological
perception' – *New Statesman*

A Certain Smile

After two blissful weeks with the man she loved . . .

'I wanted to repeat that word to myself: alone,
alone. But what of it? I was a woman, and I had
loved a man. It was a simple story; there was
nothing to make a fuss about.'

In the novel which followed *Bonjour Tristesse* a
young girl enters a light-hearted affair with a
married man only to find there is no more
happiness once the emotions are involved.